You're Standing in My Light

YOU'RE STANDING IN MY LIGHT

and other stories

ELEANORE DEVINE

Beacon Press

Beacon Press
25 Beacon Street
Boston, Massachusetts 02108-2800

Beacon Press books
are published under the auspices of
the Unitarian Universalist Association of Congregations.

97 96 95 94 93 92 91 90   1 2 3 4 5 6 7 8

Preparation of this book was partially supported by a grant
from the Illinois Arts Council, a state agency, and by the
National Endowment for the Arts.

Portions of this work originally appeared in the following
publications: *The Hoboken Terminal*: "Marriage Is Such a
Box"; *Indiana Review*: "Pietà," "Brotherhood"; *Kansas
Quarterly*: "Triage," "The Long Homecoming"; *Menominie
Review*: "Desiderata"; *Other Voices*: "You're Standing in My
Light," "Goodbye, Charlie," "Cooked"; *The Sun*: "Heritage
Clay."

Text design by Lisa Diercks

Library of Congress Cataloging-in-Publication Data

Devine, Eleanore.
You're standing in my light, and other stories / Eleanore Devine.
p.   cm.
Contents: Pietà—Marriage is such a box—Desiderata—You're
standing in my light—Triage—Goodbye, Charlie—Cooked—A
certain difficulty in being—The long homecoming—To the sacred
dark—Brotherhood—"I don't understand you," she said—
Heritage clay.
ISBN 0-8070-8322-4
1. Title.
PS3554.E92814Y68   1990.
813'.54—dc20   89-43075

In memory of my mother,
Mary Colt Edwards.
She hid her typewriter
in the laundry basket.

◻ **Contents** ◻

▫ Pietà ▫

. . . *worm-worn Pietàs*
reorganizing victimization . . .
—Adrienne Rich

I'd just that morning gotten my driver's license, and there I was, driving in sleet and rain at night. Mother was in the back seat, knees spread, holding Andy across her lap and singing to him. I didn't want to hear her. I didn't want to look at them. Looking hurt. I was already sitting in a puddle because of the hurt; when Mother insisted that Doctor MacKenzie and the orderly lift my brother into her lap, I shook so that blood flowed right through my Tampax.

I didn't have to turn to know how they looked. Andy, tall like Dad, limp and sprawling, wrapped in blankets and bolstered by pillows. One hundred and two pounds, his stomach swollen like one of those starving babies in Cambodia. He was wearing a tan bathrobe and underneath was a diaper. Mother, a large woman, was wearing her best blue coat, and holding her broken son like the Madonna we saw in Rome last summer.

I hate that statue. I love it.

The sleet began to freeze on the pavement and the lights along the street shone back from the dark and made me blink. Every shadow seemed another car rushing out of the blackness. I braked for a car that wasn't there. For months I'd looked forward to driving on my own; but now, all my strength seemed to pour into my eyes and hands, straining to get my mother and my brother safely home.

1

Most of all I was hoping Tom next door wouldn't see us. Tom was Andy's best friend when my brother weighed one hundred and ninety pounds, all muscle and bone and golden skin. A dimple in his left cheek. A tan crew cut. A picture-book brother until, eleven years ago, when he was sixteen. Then one shining spring morning, during a peace demonstration, a night stick dented his nose. He fell and hit his head, and everything changed for all of us.

After that, Andy began to write ten-page letters to President Nixon and Brezhnev, to Ho Chi Minh and Georges Pompidou (Andy's French was excellent), to Kissinger and U Thant, describing step by step how to stop the war. Mother used to visit Andy at Harvard until he asked her not to come any more. ("You don't understand, Mother. I want to live for people, to change America and make it ours.")

When she came home from Cambridge that last time, she said he wasn't wearing his chinos or the blue sweater she'd picked out for him because of his eyes. She said his speech was blurred. She blamed his nose, but the doctors could find nothing wrong.

The next time she heard from Andy, he was in jail. Mother got him out. He wrote Dad, "Our nation offers military answers to political and human questions." Dad wrote Andy he couldn't come home until he was a patriot like his friend Tom. Andy's next letter said, "When parents trust their children to make their own decisions, that trust cannot demand automatic adherence to the parents' values."

After that Mother didn't know where Andy was until, three years ago, the hospital in Chicago called, and she began her almost daily visits.

The car was barely moving now. I wanted to slide and slurry through the ice, to get home. What would Father do? Mother hadn't told him she was bringing Andy home.

I turned east from Green Bay Road at Kenilworth Avenue. Here, under the arching trees, I used to ride on the back of Andy's bike. The wind cut through my bones; my voice was blown away; my hair—tan like his, only long and frizzy—wrapped around my head each time Andy turned a corner. At the end of the avenue is Lake Michigan. Andy used to swim far out with me on his back. "I'll be your dolphin," he'd say. Now, the way he was, the gentle voice lost, it seemed, forever, made me wonder again if maybe it was my fault, but I'd only done what he asked. I was just a kid. "I'm so miserable," he'd say.

The trees seemed to wrap Kenilworth Avenue in darkness. The car moved inch by inch. No one's religious in our family, but I was praying, "Please, God, don't let Tom be home." Hearing Mother cry out as Andy groaned and lolled forward and she struggled to steady him, I slid through a stop sign I must have practiced a thousand times during Driver's Ed. A white Triumph with a canvas top— like a bandaged bug—backed out of a driveway. Slowly, not daring to touch the brakes, I skidded and locked bumpers with the Triumph.

Officer Tompkins was there within minutes. Pad in hand, he thrust his head through the window I'd opened for him. I couldn't speak. Mother said, "Yes, sir?" the *yes* soft and subservient, the *sir* like a whip. Tompkins hunched down and looked us over. "Mrs. Aldrich?" He put his arrest pad in his pocket.

"Officer Tompkins," she said, "I'm taking my son home to die." The policeman jumped on our bumper until the cars were free. Then he led the way up Essex Road.

Our house seemed small under the elms, dimly white and withdrawn. Ice had formed on each tree limb. The wind fretted them. They moved slowly, moaning. Each twig seemed to cry out in a small, high voice. Father came to the door. "Mary, Mary," he said, "I've worried about you."

He usually calls Mother Bess, which gets us mixed up

because my name is Beth. There was a half-empty glass in Dad's hand. He was still in his office suit—thin striped, a wider stripe to the shirt and tie. "Mary," he said, "the children are hungry."

He put down his glass and turned on the porch light. The house leapt into warmth. The burning bush by the tilted square porch, ice on every branch, sparkled in the light. The stucco of the house gleamed. He steadied himself on the curved iron handrail and came down the stairs. When he saw Andy, he made a choked sound. He leaned in and took Andy from Mother's arms. Dad's hands, rigid as if they too were frozen, clutched Andy, pulling at him. Dad stumbled on the steps. Out of the dimness between our house and the one next door stepped Tom. He tossed that perpetual black cigar of his over his shoulder and said, "Let me help you, sir."

Our five-year-old twins, Jerry and Jill, were standing at the top of the stairs as Tom carried Andy up to his old room. Dad followed murmuring something I couldn't hear. His face seemed to break in shreds, jagged yet swollen. He looked incredibly old. In Andy's room, we all watched Tom put Andy to bed. He was home again. I went to see if my coat were stained.

My mother has this pietà complex. *Complex* is my grandmother's word. She says that when she was growing up, everyone had one: Inferiority complex. Messiah complex. Oedipus complex. No one but Mother could collect so many miserable people in Kenilworth. Bettsy who calls every morning to say she hasn't slept and why. Janey who drinks. Her husband made her get up one morning at 4:15 and take a shower. He said, "I want you clean before I kiss you." Marion whose nine-year-old steals her Equanil. Barbara who's got a job she loves but can't keep a housekeeper; her husband often moves to the University Club. Tom's mother who comes over regularly to tell Mother she's afraid Tom will never get over the war and find a proper job. And, of course, my father.

My father is treasurer for a fine, small publishing company. He still pays the employees personally in cash each Friday. Dad says the president is paranoid. He reads Dad's mail and marks it with suggestions and corrections. "His syntax," Dad says, "is deplorable."

Mother knows the moment Dad gets out of his car whether he's miserable or not, and if he is, she sets up what we kids call the candlelight service. She feeds us in the kitchen, makes Dad a Gibson, double, and lights the candles in the dining room. All through dinner, she pats Dad's hand and says, "Yes, yes." She does the same when Dad shouts about the Russians or the Iranians. She knows he doesn't want her to say anything. Mother can find good in everyone. She even forgives Caligula. "Caligula's mother," she says, "was . . . ," and Dad says, "And what about *her* mother?" and Mother says, "That's what's so sad, John. Generation after generation . . ."

None of my mother's friends set up candlelight services, although some of them still have that dear-little-woman tic. They smile and nod as their men talk. They probably aren't listening. I think most husbands expect bastard bosses. Most husbands go out and hit golf balls or jog. They go to meetings and holler and drink. I think it's Mother's fault my father is miserable. He's never learned to deal with his feelings.

Mother hugs everyone. Dad still hugs Mother, but I doubt that even the night the twins were conceived he stopped telling her about the office troubles or bombing some country off the map.

It's only fair to say that for all this pietà stuff, Mother never forgets us kids. She calls the twins "my happy afterthought." She's so good I sometimes hate her. I think it's because she's always right.

My counselor at New Trier is just a little older than Andy

and Tom. She says my trouble is that I don't like any of my role models. She suggests Mother Jones, Emma Goldman, or Emily Dickinson. She also says I've got to separate thinking from feeling before I go to Smith. She's never married. (That's Mother's phrase.) She told me once that something happened to the men in her generation. "I've had plenty of men ask me to marry them," she said, "but they all want me to take care of *them*." She called them "the walking wounded."

Dad was good with Andy, but day by day, Dad seemed to get thinner and whiter. Sometimes when Mother was sitting by Andy's bed, my father would come in and say, "The latest news from Iran is . . . ," and she would say, "Not now, dear." Dad's face would turn whiter still and he'd go downstairs and make his own Gibson. He used to bring his drink up to my room where I'd gone to hide from the TV and the constant news bulletins. He'd tell me about the hostages until I learned to say, "I can't listen now, Dad. I've got to study."

It took Andy six months to die. All through those months, I came straight home from school in the afternoon. I dropped my modern dance class. I stopped going to school parties. I hated what Mother was doing, but I knew she was right and that I should help.

Our old friend Doctor MacKenzie came regularly. It was Doctor Mac who'd helped Mother get Andy released from the hospital. Each time he came, he said, "Keep him warm and comfortable. There's not much we can do." The twins carried trays to Andy's room. The neighbors made casseroles. (Bettsy's was burned.) The cleaning woman came twice a week. Dad took several days' vacation and found a nurse for Andy, but Mother fired her. She said, "He's my son."

Mother grew deeper, sadder, yet somehow larger, holding us all together, being a mother, living on the memory of strength and the admiration of her friends. Smiling so Andy would know she wanted him home. There were no more candlelight services. She and Dad never touched. I lived to a new refrain. "Never. Never. Never for me."

I was full of myself and my hopes, missing my friends at school, the class offices I might have had, the dates that might have happened if I'd gone to some of the parties. Friends still came, but mostly they talked to Mother. I was lonely, yet I kept telling myself that the only way to get anything done was to be lonely. One of my problems was that I didn't know what I wanted to do except to go away to college and live a while for myself.

One day, coming home from school, I found Mother waiting for me on the upper landing near Andy's room. She didn't speak for a long time. She just held me and I held her. Then she said, "Beth, please, try and look more pleasant. Andy's not in pain. He knows he's home." And then, reaching deep inside somewhere for that smile of hers, she said, "I've been wanting to tell you. You have such a beautiful smile. I want you to hang on to that smile for Smith."

I didn't cry. I went for a walk down to the beach. I shouted, "Shit. Shit. Shit," at the lake until the tears came.

I sat by Andy's bed a lot. I held his hand—thin bones, like a claw, the brown faded to a dirty yellow—and remembered how I'd held his penis all those years ago, Andy saying, "I'm so miserable." I wasn't smart enough then to say, "You learned that I'm-so-miserable trick from Dad."

I knew now I hadn't done anything wrong. Andy had asked. I just wished that before his injury, when he was still thinking well, when he could still speak, I'd been old enough to understand what he was saying, to march with him, to go to jail with him. One of his sentences I did remember: "A citizen in a democracy has to protest when his country is wrong."

Tom helped. I had not expected him to. He was still working as an orderly at the hospital, and when he'd finished there and had his dinner, he'd come over from next door and give Andy a bath. In the night, when Mother couldn't restrain Andy, Tom seemed to know. He always came. Afterwards, as Mother dozed by Andy's bed, Tom and I would sit by the fire in the darkened living room and he'd talk, one foot turning clockwise, then counterclockwise.

He told me he'd struck Andy in the face, again and again, because of the war. "He wouldn't hit back," Tom said. "I hated him. He was always so right—so righteous. Andy said, 'Keep sitting on your ideals like Simon Stylites, and the bully boys will have us propping up dominoes, worldwide.' He said, 'Let's make sense of America.' He said, 'Come, burn your draft card and follow me.'

"I hated his face. Mine was like an old volcano cone then. He had all those muscles. And a mother who listened to him . . . Beth, I just kept hitting him, hitting him because he was so sure he was right."

Tom is about my size. His face is smooth now, still young. His hair is pale and pulled back in a ponytail. "The last male ponytail in Kenilworth," I called it. "One less head of hair to blow dry," he'd say. "All that energy going into hot air."

Tom never looked at me as he talked. He stared into the fire. That same night he told me about hitting Andy, he started telling me about the war. The burning huts. The burning people. "I did it too," he said. "We had to. But sometimes we did it when we didn't need to." Over and over, night after night, he told me. On and on he told me, until I felt my energy for school and for college seep away like blood.

There by the fire, Tom said, "I wish I could tell Andy it's all right. When I hold him, bathing him, I say over and over, 'It's all right, kid. We both did what we thought we had to do.' "

Sometimes when Andy slept, Mother would come downstairs and sit with us. Tom went right on talking about the war, but for Mother he'd remember the funny things: the rainy day he'd marched up and saluted an officer, slipped, and kept on slipping, sliding on his bottom until he knocked over the officer. The time one hundred and ten men got sick at exactly the same moment after eating turkey that had been roasted one day and reheated the next.

It was as if he trusted only me with the really bad stories. That pleased me. For a while.

Andy died in late March. The autopsy showed a seepage from the brain.

Most evenings Tom still came. I wondered why. He still talked and talked about the war. One cool night in April I said, "I'd like to tell you about the paper I'm writing. It's about aesthetics." He listened, but my words felt hollow and unreal. "You're a smart girl," he said. He didn't ask any questions. He went back to telling about the war. He was still a POW, held captive not only by the bad things he'd seen, but by the memory of what his friends had done, what he had done, from boredom or anger or fear.

I moved down to the rug by the fire. "Never again," I said.

"Never what?"

"I don't want to hear about the war again." I knew the stories, even the story about the young lieutenant just out from the States who was gang raped. I didn't have the strength to feel them again. "Women spend their lives listening to men," I said.

"Do they now?" he said. "Mind if I smoke?"

This was one of our jokes. I always said no, but he knew

I hated that big black cigar. I understood. I'd heard about that too. He'd told me about the heroin, about the day in Amsterdam when he'd heard about the bombing of Cambodia and said, "I'm wasting my life." He'd had his friends lock him in his room. He made them promise they wouldn't let him out no matter what he said or did. I could almost hear the screaming. Smell the vomit. I knew about the swearing. I knew that his friends kept their promise and that now, when he remembered, he smoked that filthy cigar.

The fire was dwindling. Upstairs all was quiet. Mother and Dad were together again in their big bed. At least, I hoped so. Tom moved closer. "I think you've got it turned around," he said. "I thought it was women and men helping each other."

There was silence then, there by the fire, the sparks rising, the last log glowing softly, the sh-sh-sh of the furnace purring through the darkened room, spring almost come, so that for a while there would be no more fires. The warmth of Tom beside me gave me a feeling I'd never known. All the loneliness of the winter rose up and made me soft and warm and defenseless. He lay down and put his head in my lap. My fingers slid down that silly ponytail. It felt like straw. He had the longest eyelashes I'd ever seen. I tried to close my knees, but of course I couldn't with his head there.

"Beth," he said, "I need you. I'm so miserable." For a moment I thought he'd called me Bess, as if it weren't true that I didn't have to be like Mother.

I couldn't move. Something like gentleness seeped through my bones. I leaned down to him and my fingers traced his eyebrows. The log fell. Sparks flew upward. The fire faded. Tom moved away from me, and for a brief time I thought maybe he knew I'd promised myself, "Never.

Never. Never for me." But, no, he crouched on his knees and put his arms around me. His lips were on mine. I wasn't sure I could, but I pulled away. I said, "Not when you're miserable."

□

■ Marriage Is Such a Box ■

That first day we stopped for lunch at Nashville House; Zoë took the box in with her.

Friends since freshman year at New Trier High School, the three of us were on what we long ago dubbed our sanity trip, our biennial vacation from the bliss of suburban marriage. As we each buttered our second baking powder biscuit, Harriet said, "Phil read my first copy of NOW and moved to the guest room."

"Lysistrata's uncle?" I asked.

"He says he can't. Because I joined NOW."

I asked, "You aren't going to give in, are you?"

"Can't is can't. ERA is ERA."

Zoë in her pale blue suit—she was doing her mourning in blue—shook her head. "Surely a marriage counts more than principle."

Firelight glinted on copper kettles. A fly, alerted by spring, attacked the apple butter. Outside, a shovel scraped at unexpected snow. Beside Zoë, on the fourth chair, was the box. Teak with shining copper clasps. Already it was beginning to annoy me. Her damned diamonds, no doubt.

Finally Harriet said, "It hurts. After all these years."

We did not know it then, but this was to be the last of our trips together, and it was turning into a female hotline, twenty-four-hour service. Harriet and I had planned it quite differently. We intended to do everything we could to ease Zoë, who in December had lost her husband, Dag, and their best friend, Harold, in a completely avoidable boating accident.

Harriet and I almost had a tiff over how to help Zoë. "Marion," Harriet had said, "just don't be cheery all the time. You'll depress her."

Now, Harriet helped herself to another biscuit from the calico-skirted basket. A thumb, sticky with the famous honey touched my hand. "Phil says you're the one who talked me into joining."

"Oh, no. It was old Bob-o."

Old Bob-o is my husband. A good LaSalle Street lawyer, even if he is soft on fees. He is not old at all; he is my age.

Back on Universal Highway 65, Zoë sat in back again, one leg up to ease the ache that still persisted from a long ago egg beater down the slopes of Aspen. The box was in her lap.

As usual, Harriet, all breast and bottom and Botticelli smile, was driving and talking. At home she answered the telephone with, "Guess what happened to me." Her husband would take out his watch and say, "I'll give you five minutes."

Now she was saying, "Since Phil abandoned my bed, men tell me dirty jokes. I've had three invitations to lunch. Me. At sixty."

On our trips Harriet always talked like a gramophone gone wild. I smoked more than usual until my operation. Zoë wore her glasses and read most of the night. Year after year, we broke all the travel rules our husbands had taught us. We chattered before breakfast, were silent after lunch, never discussed spark plugs or cars that passed on the right. We drank more than we did at home and laughed when we got lost.

In the early days, we talked about flowers and scenery and all the good things in our lives. Then, with Vietnam, drugs among the young, and my weekly colostomy support group, we began our reality talks. Why Harriet's daughter got pregnant on purpose at Mount Holyoke. Why my eldest son ran out of gas three times on his way back to Brown from Smith. (The police picked him up, red gasoline can in hand, walking the white dividing line on the highway.)

Zoë never had problems to report. She claimed her marriage was perfect. Her sons, adopted because Dag did not want her to risk her figure or her health, never seemed to do anything but get on the dean's list at Yale, pledge Bones, marry girls with old-money grandfathers, and in due course, father sons who appeared to have been born in alligator shirts.

During our reality period, Harriet stopped writing novels about near rape. (She could not bear to have anything bad happen to her heroines. She called her unsold novels "my almost series.") She began to write and sell magazine interviews about people in crisis. That was the time I gave up cookies and cakes and the PTA and, with Bob's encouragement, helped found a women's center.

Now, a horn sounded. Harriet combed tapered fingers through short gray curls that bounced as she talked. She returned her hands to the wheel and guided the car back into the right lane. A car passed. The driver gave her the finger. She said, "It's not bad having a bed to myself." Her tone belied every word.

I had been thinking it would be good to roll into bed without being reminded of the smudge on the front door and the leaky tap in the basement.

"I'd miss Bob," I said.

"The saddest words," Zoë said.

Before I could answer, Harriet said, "Anyone who talks as much as I do is bound to say something stupid once an hour."

Sooner or later, and usually sooner, Harriet realizes what she has said. Last week I heard her tell the wife of a one-legged man, "Women who marry cripples have weak egos."

I was turning as clumsy of tongue as Harriet, both of us

talking to Zoë about husbands and beds.

"Zoë," I said, trying to make amends, "there's room on the floor for your box."

Zoë always traveled in pastels. Soft colors went well with the hair I once described to Bob as "one-hundred-dollar red—one hundred dollars a week." My hair and Harriet's grew fainter with the years; Zoë's grew brighter.

Zoë always looked perfect in her pastels, but they did make for excess luggage. And now, the box.

"I want to hold it," Zoë said. It was like her to travel with her diamonds.

"You should have left them in the vault," Harriet said. "Oh, no."

Who but Dag would have given his wife a diamond on every occasion and expected her to wear as many as possible at all times? Dag sent diamonds for the anniversary of their first kiss, their wedding, her birthday, and the birthdays of the two adopted boys. It was the diamonds for the kids that sometimes made me snap at Bob. I had eight-and-a-half months of vomit for each of our five kids. I would not have missed a day of it for a cradle-sized diamond. Still, I sometimes forgot I did not like diamonds.

One morning, early, before we left on this trip, Bob had told me that after Dag died Zoë could not find any insurance, or bank accounts. "The house and the diamonds will take care of her for a while," Bob said. "And Harold . . . Wall Street seems to have cleaned out Harold."

Later he called from the office to remind me that a client's confidences are sacred. I hung up in midsentence. I had not been a lawyer's wife for thirty-eight years for nothing. Three hours later a florist delivered a dozen red roses. Bob's note said, "I paid our insurance premium this morning."

I almost lost my temper with Zoë when we stopped for the night. I opened the door for her. Slowly she swung her ski leg down from the seat and slid toward me. I held out my hand for the box.

She said, "I can hold it."

"Just till you get out."

She pushed me away so hard I almost fell. She took the box to dinner with her.

The next morning, south of Louisville, daffodils and hyacinths bloomed. The hills swelled like sleeping cats. The earth was red. We passed a country graveyard washed bright by the night's rain. I did not ask Harriet to stop so I could do some of the rubbings Bob likes; nor did I mention the white crosses by the roadside.

Instead I read tollgate signs. "No exit without exact change." "No exit after 65."

"Five years to decide what to do," Harriet said.

Then, after a long pause: "Marriage is such a box. I didn't mean to tell you."

Later she said, "I still love him a lot. I hate drying up like an old lady. Ashes to ashes. Dust to . . ."

I said, "Shut up, Harriet."

Quickly she tried to interest Zoë in the battlefields we were going to visit. Orchard Knob. Signal Point.

I stopped listening. I hate war talk. It does not matter what war. At Signal Point I planned to wander off and look for tadpoles and bunny babies.

Zoë did not respond to Harriet, but then she seldom did except with a smile and an "Oh?" Everyone always centered his words and actions on Zoë. At parties she stationed herself in a big chair that complemented the sapphire or misty green or pale blue of her dress and smiled and ohed. All evening the guests would circle her. The women would bring food. The men would bring her compliments and their best *bons mots,* simplified, Bob said, so she could understand.

Dag would call her "mybeautifulZoë," making it one word. Year after year, she had grown more beautiful for him despite a long scar on her forehead from a tumble the first time he took her riding.

Dag. Even in death he was as much a part of our trip as had ever been. I had thought at first that Dag could not be his real name. It sounded too much like a comic strip hero. Or one of those wish-fullfillment males in mystery novels who never say no to an eager woman. Not only was it his name, it was his Scandinavian heritage. Dag, our Dag, Zoë's Dag, was Dag the Fourth.

I especially remember one party just before Dag and Harold died. All evening people kept calling me to the kitchen. "Please come. We need you." Even our babysitter—we have a sitter for my mother now that the kids have finally moved out—telephoned to tell me a toilet was overflowing.

Meanwhile, there was Madame Récamier–Zoë, Dag and Harold bringing her vermouth on ice (on trips she drank bourbon), and playing the party for her like a tennis match. I asked Harriet's husband how Zoë did it.

"She listens," he said.

Later, warm in Bob's arms, I said, "That Zoë. Our very own bonfire of sex."

"You said last week she had plastic perfection. The week before, you said she was a cool stream men like to go wading in."

"Warming everyone with her smile." Sometimes when I am mixing my metaphors I ignore Bob.

"Harold needs warming," Bob said. "I've never seen such a pale man."

"It can't be easy, being a bachelor with only an adopted family. Even if that family is Dag and Zoë."

"I'm glad I have my own family. Now, how about some milk and graham crackers?"

"She doesn't even like to ski. Or sail," I said. "She'd rather go on a Caribbean cruise and watch the water go by."

"Sometimes she gets to stay back at the lodge with Harold."

"I don't approve. Pretending to like sports just for Dag. But she's got guts."

"My gut's demanding graham crackers."

"It's cold out there."

I was halfway out of bed when he added, "Bonfire."

Serving the milk and crackers, I said, "What some women will do to please their men."

"Hmmmmmm."

At our house milk and grahams after love mean, "That was good." Bob's special gift to me was making loving good again after my operation.

Zoë had always insisted that she could not leave Dag for our trips; yet, at the last moment, she came along. Harriet said it was good for Zoë to get away from Dag's constant praise. Zoë spent a lot of time in beauty parlors, reducing salons, and dress shops, trying to be perfect for Dag. If ever in a distraught moment—for even Zoë had times of doubt—she discovered her bra and panties did not match, she would disrobe and dress again. Properly. Sometimes, knees muddy from scrubbing floors or weeding gardens, I could not decide whether I envied or pitied her perfection.

Dag loved her for it. He dedicated his life to making her happy. He was always planning trips abroad for her—ski trips and walking tours, even after she hurt her leg. Spontaneous trips were his specialty. We learned long ago not to count on Dag and Zoë for parties; still the parties they did attend were the gayest. Harold came with them, even if the hostess had forgotten to invite him.

Bob used to say that Dag never went anywhere without Harold because Harold was such a perfect foil for him. Small, with the look of an old leatherbound book.

We had not been on the road more than three hours, that

second day of our last trip together, when Harriet suddenly turned off the highway. "Let's get lost," she said.

Even Zoë laughed.

"Maybe we'll end up in Mississippi," she said.

Years ago, before the highways, before the Ramada Inns, we got lost in Mississippi and had to stay in a drafty cabin left over from *It Happened One Night*. Zoë put on a peach-colored cashmere sweater and fuchsia wool stretch pants under her fawn-colored marabou-trimmed negligée. We raised our bourbon glasses, "To perfection," and laughed ourselves to sleep on lumpy mattresses that smelled of Flit. The next morning we marched around the kidney-hued court house up the road as if it were a national monument.

Now, on a side road, just north of Murfreesboro, I spoke quietly. "Car on the right."

Harriet turned the wheel just as a 1949 Marathon cut in from a side road. Our car plunged off the road and jumped a small incline. In the Marathon an old man with a face like a dirty work glove gunned the motor and rattled away. Zoë gasped and slid off the back seat.

"Another adventure." Harriet flipped her curls. I laughed, but it was a duty laugh.

The car showed no damage, but the right wheel was lodged behind a red stone. No one asked who would go for help. I am the one who goes. That is why I travel barelegged in a washable skirt and tennis shoes. Harriet spread a blanket on a log for Zoë.

"I'll sit here and look at the forsythia," Zoë said. "Just think. Still snow on my compost pile."

"Me for the shade." Harriet pulled a book from her purse. Blessedly she did not remind Zoë that she lived in an apartment now and no longer had a garden, a gardener, or a compost pile.

Three miles down the road I found a farmer to jack up the wheel. It was only when we were ready to leave, the farmer thanked, and information on Civil War monuments in the neighborhood exchanged, that I heard Zoë sob. "My box."

Harriet kept pushing her dark glasses into the red grooves on her nose as she searched the car. My colostomy bag grumbled. (Sometimes it gurgles so loudly I'm sure everyone can hear it. Once in church it smelled. The priest came along just in time, swinging his incense. Incense. One good reason to be Catholic.) It did not take me long to find the box behind the log where Zoë had rested. It was heavier than I expected. I did not call out my discovery, but slid my fingers along the teak and flipped the rococo lock with my thumb. Inside was a plastic box. There were no velvet envelopes suitable for diamonds, only this stuff, white and gritty. Zoë, I remembered, had slept with the box the night before.

I carried it to her, trying to pretend I was not touching it. Her cheeks were ashen. The faint eyeliner she still used seemed garish.

The road back to the turnpike twisted through low mountains. Trees stood like bristles in a hairbrush, each branch distinct against the strong blue of the sky.

"More lambs this way," I said. I did not want to think about what I had seen.

"GET RIGHT WITH GOD." "TEN MILES WORLD FAMOUS PE-CAN ROLLS." I called out the signs along the way. Red birdhouses with peaked roofs commanded, "SEE ROCK CITY."

"Six turtles on a log," I reported. Actually there were four, but six sounded better.

"Dammit, stop being so cheerful," Harriet said.

At a turn in the road was a small clearing. Red cliffs lowered over the charred remains of a house. Three brick chimneys rose forlorn. The house must once have faced the morning sun. There was still a terrace bright with daffodils.

"Stop," Zoë said. "Oh, please, let's stop."

The flowers seemed to grow wild; but a loving hand had set them to a pattern. Zoë knelt among the yellow flowers. She began to cry, softly at first, then openly, helplessly, not wiping away the tears. "It must have been perfect here," she said. "Now everything's gone."

I held her close. "Cry," I said.

"Our life was perfect too," she said. "I was brought up to believe a woman must make marriage perfect."

"We all miss Dag," Harriet said.

I thought about Bob and wished I would learn not to begrudge him his right to fuss about downspouts and what is going to happen to Social Security before we are old enough to get some.

"You had a perfect marriage," Harriet was saying.

"It had to be perfect," Zoë said. "Dag was so disappointed if I fell . . . or failed." Now the words came unheeded. "We didn't make love on our honeymoon. For a week. . . . Dag didn't follow an order on Iwo and . . . When he came home his brothers intended to keep running the business without him." Before our eyes she had turned transparent.

"Dag used to say to Harold, 'I'll catch up. I'll catch up.' And Harold would say, 'Accept what you are. Enjoy what you are.' Then I would cry and Dag would be angry with me, and Harold would be angry with him. Dag would pound the wall and shout, 'I want to lead the parade.' Then Harold would be sad and say, 'You have a perfect marriage. I don't even have that.' It was Harold who made sure Dag made money."

Suddenly Zoë was on her feet, moving back and forth with a swiftness we had not seen since her ski accident. She ripped daffodils from the once-loved beds until her arms were full. The crimped red edges of the flowers, bright against the yellow, were so crisp they seemed synthetic. Zoë's hair fell over her shoulders as she toiled up the low terrace. Her face turned to crinkle crepe as she paced the ashes of the ruins, hurling yellow flowers at the stark chimneys. Her high heels bit into the charred floorboards, raising clouds of black ash. The green stems of the daffodils, juicy and bright, popped as she stamped on them. For one short malicious moment, I almost followed with her damn box, sprinkling whatever it contained among the daffodils. Harriet held me back and we stood, unable to speak, until a tickling in my hand made me look down. Harriet's nails had drawn blood.

We helped Zoë to the car. Juice from the jonquil stems spotted her blue dress. One green leaf stuck to a pale blue shoe. I put the box in her lap.

"You were lucky in your marriage," Harriet said. "We all were. No matter what happened. We forget."

"It was perfect."

"Sometimes we forget," Harriet said.

I held Zoë close but she seemed far away. "He's always with me," she said at last. Her fingers caressed the box in her lap.

"The box?" I said. "Dag?"

"Yes," she said quite clearly. "And Harold."

April, 1983. We are not traveling together this spring.

Harriet is living in a women's commune in Vermont with her daughter and her child.

Zoë is at the Lake Shore Health Residence. In fair weather she sits on her balcony beside the lake. She thinks she is on a Caribbean cruise.

I will not be going anywhere for a while. Last week I changed a tire on Edens Expressway. Bob kept telling me, "Everyone who is for ERA should learn to change a tire." So I did.

□

◻ Desiderata ◻

On this late fall afternoon, Annie Goode is in her back yard among the drifting oak leaves, attacking the compost pile as if that were her problem. She digs deeper, pretending all the while that her need is trivial. Next door, beyond the high hedge, a lawn mower growls as Hank, her best friend's husband, gives his lawn its final fall cutting.

She pushes the barrow toward the flower beds and tries to ignore the tremor that has given new rhythm to her days and nights. Atop the dirt in her wheelbarrow an earthworm rises and shakes its fat self. Annie feels betrayed by her good habits: Daily walks. Weekly swims. Vitamins except E. No more coffee. No more tea. Only her husband's second-hand nicotine. She still drinks, sometimes late at night alone at the kitchen table. Like Mark Twain, she and her best friend, Jeanne, are saving one bad habit to throw overboard in case of dire disease.

Her gravest mistake was yesterday's giggle. Just this once she cannot go through the hedge and talk it out with Jeanne.

Her friend's hair is blonde to please her husband. Annie's is gray. Her friend's every sentence still begins with her husband's name. "Hank says." "Hank's buying a bigger sailboat." "Hank's planning a trip to the Out Islands. Hank will expect me to scuba all day and make love all night. Hank clocks himself, Annie; I truly believe he's trying to make a new record, and, frankly, I'm tired."

Annie thinks of the night ahead and shovels faster. There is still time before sunset to top-dress her tulip bed.

Four-year-old David, who lives three houses west, cuts through the yard. She puts down her shovel and waits for him. Baseball cap turned backwards, jeans flapping at the knees, he scowls as he presents a muddy hand. His eyes stare directly into hers as he has been taught. On the sidewalk beyond Annie's chrysanthemums, the boy's mother stops the baby carriage and spells it out for Annie: "SIBLING RIVALRY." Annie squeezes David's hand. When he is sorrowful, he shakes her hand. On his happy days, he hugs her.

It's time to go in and start dinner. Time to find Bear sitting in her grandmother's chair in front of the TV, a circle of burns on the carpet at his feet from pipes and cigarettes dropped as he dozed. Their two daughters often speak of him as "Our Father Arthur Cunningham Goode." He may have been, before his reluctant retirement two years ago at seventy-five, the scourge of Chicago's slum lords, but for Annie he has always been a Teddy bear. As for Annie, now sixty-two, their friends still speak of her as "Arthur's young wife."

She can hear the blat of the evening news. Inside, she knows, the house shakes and shrieks. She does not want to go in, yet somewhere a voice calls, "Hurry." Maybe Bear needs her. Two years ago when she sold her shares in a feminist bookstore, she said, "Bear needs me at home."

She returns the wheelbarrow to the garage and notes with pleasure the trim rows of pots and implements she cleaned yesterday morning. A new shriek cuts the cooling air. The mower next door stops. Hank comes through the hedge. He is tall and shambling and his bones show. He wears designer jeans and a Brooks shirt. She waves, shaking her head. For the first time in forty years, she does not want to talk to Hank.

He blocks her way. "Jeanne's off downstate to see her father. Nurse trouble. What're you doing for dinner?"

This question can be interpreted two ways. "How about inviting me to dinner?" or "How about dinner with me?"

She says, "Not tonight."

"When?" he calls as she hurries toward the rambling gray stucco house.

Hank's insistence is her fault. *Mea culpa. Mea* giggle. Yesterday at a wedding reception.

"It's good to dance again," he said.

"Jeanne dances."

"Well . . ."

His hand caressed the slimness of her stomach, releasing that unforgivable giggle. She pulled away, but Hank knew. All these years. Dancing. Arguing late at night over drinks. Reality versus idealism. Sooner or later he always said, "You're the only one I know who still cares what happens to the world." Once he called her "blessedly naive," and their friendship survived. She sat with him at the hospital during the long hours of Jeanne's last birth. They walked together all day while Bear was in surgery.

"Hank," she said as she moved away. "You're getting to be an old patter."

"I'll buy that."

Deftly his hand moved down and under.

Now she runs, pulling off her garden gloves in the kitchen; she smells smoke. In the study, Bear flaps his large-print *Times* at his flaming armchair. His striped tie still nestles neatly in the curve of his gray pullover sweater. Only his English brogues, which he refuses to replace, show strain. A toe emerges from the splintered left shoe.

"Annie, my dear," he says. "I think it would be advisable to call the fire department."

The flames shoot straight up. The smoke thickens. Still flapping the paper, slowly now, more in annoyance than in hopes of putting out the flames, he peers through the smoke at the TV. Dan Rather is announcing a national crisis.

Annie runs for a bucket of water. She pushes Bear aside and pours water over the chair. The flames dwindle, then spurt up again. She goes to refill the bucket. Blackened water drips on the scarred carpet. The smell of goose-down scorches the air. The chair smoulders. Bear pushes the TV into a far corner and continues to watch Rather. The paper flutters aimlessly behind his back. Small flames circle the chair. She steps on them, one by one.

Taking his newspaper, she turns him back to the chair. "Out," she says. His brows crumple in a frown, as if to say, "Really, there's no need to interrupt," but he helps her push the chair through the kitchen and out the door into the yard.

Hank comes running. She says, "Everything under control. No fire department."

Hank says, "Are you sure?" His fingers touch her arm. She slips away.

Before dinner, as always, Annie accepts the double martini Bear has carefully measured for her. Two parts gin. One part vermouth. An old-fashioned martini in the glass he set to frost just after lunch. "To my loveliest," he says with a small bow. She raises her glass to him. He sips. She nods. On the way to serve dinner she helps herself to extra gin from the bottle.

At dinner she waits for him to pull out her chair, and, as he has for all the years of their marriage, kiss the top of her head. He picks up his fork and opens his favorite book on Clarence Darrow. He eats greedily. Annie forces herself to cut her lamb chops into small pieces and to put down her fork after each bite.

She says, "I can't be as hungry as I am." Bear does not answer.

Midway through dinner he says, "I could have eaten a potato."

She does not say, "I burned the potatoes." It has been years since she last burned their food.

In the kitchen their after-dinner decaf is percolating.

Their silent meal done (Annie long ago insisted, "No TV during dinner"), he goes to his corner in the living room, pulls the extra-bright light close, and with a large magnifying glass continues to read. She stays in the kitchen and cleans a cupboard. A box of spaghetti spills like jackstraws across the floor. She picks them up, one by one.

Later she sits by the window at the far side of the large living room. Her favorite lamp is there. Her sewing box. Her books. She can look out the window and wave at her friends. She picks up her needlepoint. She has given up knitting; in this last year she has knitted more sweaters, socks, and caps than their daughters and their children will ever wear. She counts on eight seat covers to keep her hands busy this winter.

She threads a needle with gray wool, looks across at her husband. There are new shadows under his eyes. She is sure he is in pain. She can almost see the bones go crisp and the blood thin, but it would be useless to ask the doctor to come again. Bear would thank him for coming, offer a martini, refuse to answer questions, and tell him about Darrow and Altgeld. All she can do is watch him more closely.

Slowly Annie pushes her needle through the heavy canvas seat-backing. Winter is coming. Time to stay home. Time to give up the rest of her committees. (In this town she is friend to every closet feminist with a checkbook.) Each day she feels one more door closing. No more theater or concerts with Bear. No more walking for peace. Bear never did like any form of exercise, but he used to walk with her if it were *for* something. Only once has he refused to march or carry a banner. "We need nuclear energy," he said.

She puts down her needlework and scrutinizes the living room. Her engagement picture stands on the big old desk that had once been her great-grandfather's. "Arthur's so old," her mother had said. Father had responded, "Big deal. When Annie's seventy and wants to go to the Stork Club, Arthur will be eighty-five and want to stay home and read." There was still a Stork Club the year of her engagement.

Making lists in her head of all that needs to be done, Annie is glad once more that she did not follow Jeanne's lead—Hank insisted—and get rid of the family furniture. The old pieces gleam with lemon oil. The chintzes are fresh, but the windows have not been washed on the outside since Bear's retirement. Getting up on a ladder is one thing Annie no longer enjoys. To the left of the fireplace is a deep gash where number two grandson ran his tricycle into the plaster. Bear's special delight may once have been to sue a landlord for not maintaining a building, but now, whenever Annie hires a handyman, Bear asks what she is paying and fires him.

Annie jabs the needle into her work, impaling a finger. Sucking the small wound, she looks out the window. Hank in his red jogging suit and blue running shoes with orange laces is standing by the streetlight. He gives her a jaunty salute and beckons. She pretends not to notice and calls out, "Bear?"

He does not answer.

"BEAR?"

He raises his heavy black eyebrows. His finger marks the word where she interrupted. He is still handsome. Barrel-chested. Bear-like. The black hair is scarcely touched with white. The dark eyes are still deep, but misted.

She goes to him and strokes his hand, touches his hair with a slim finger. "Tomorrow, Bear, let's go out for dinner."

He shakes his head. She does not know if he is rejecting

her suggestion. Perhaps he did not hear. He says, "Have I remembered, my dear, to tell you today that you have the figure of a girl?"

She leans down and kisses him, remembering the years he came home three days a week for lunch and love. Unbidden, an old story comes back to her. A Chicago heiress—Annie has forgotten her name. She only remembers that the woman was said to have seduced her black chauffeur. The family put her away, as the saying was then. Scrubbing floors was the prescribed therapy.

"Tomorrow," Annie tells Bear, "tomorrow, I'm going to wash those windows."

At ten—it seems hours later even though she has only filled twelve rows of stitches—he returns to his study. Again the house wakes to the clamor of voices and commercial jingles. Usually she joins him for the late news. Tonight she cannot risk tears as sleek and shining men and women swoon in sweet orgasm as they pour a glass of orange juice or hold hands, nuzzle, and touch in celebration of creams that remove the brown spots of age.

She turns off her light, puts up the chain at the front door, and empties the ashtray beside Bear's reading lamp. Time for bed. She stops a sigh. She never could abide women who sigh. In bed the throbbing grows worse. To the empty bedroom she says, "Maybe I should try a singles bar. The young people would love me. Or buy a bikini and go on a cruise." This is as far as she will allow her fantasies to go.

She knows what to do. In her shop were many books in which women who describe themselves as randy tell, stroke by stroke. Their younger daughter once said, "No need to let yourself go dry." Annie reaches for her book. She is rereading *Tell Me a Riddle*.

At eleven she hears his heavy step on the stair, hears his water flow in the bathroom, feels the bed sag as he lies beside her. She moves close and holds his unresponsive body for a moment, leans over a thin, jutting shoulder, misses his mouth, and kisses his ear. "Annie," he whispers, "I'm sorry."

Silently, as if silence matters, she leaves the bed. She empties the ashtrays in the study. She checks the carpet for sparks. She runs her hand over the gray brocade of the chair newly placed in front of the TV. This is her last duty of the day: to make sure nothing bursts into flame. "This incalescent house," she says to the silence. Incalescent used to be one of Bear's words for her. He loves words like incalescent, oxymoron, inacoustic, viscous, scud.

On the desk beside her engagement picture is a pewter pitcher filled with chrysanthemums. She pulls off a fading blossom, drops it in the wastebasket, and turns off the lights. In the dark she begins to walk back and forth. The house still reeks of burned feathers and scorched potatoes. The doorbell rings. For a moment she thinks, "Too late for company." Then, "Someone might need me." She leaves the chain in place and flicks on the porch light. The macramé hanging their younger daughter made for her sways as she opens the door. It is Hank. His red jogging suit is unzipped to the waist. His lips are half open. Soft.

"Annie, come walk. The moon."

"Not tonight."

"Annie, please."

His khaki hair is fluffed to cover a small balding spot. She sees the strong cheek bones. The lean jaw. The jutting nose. The asking.

"Annie," he says.

The familiar throbbing deepens. She says, "But, Hank, it has nothing to do with you."

Somewhere in the night a child is crying. Is it David, David who sleeps in his Cubs cap, David whose hugs she misses on his unhappy days? She closes and double-locks the door.

◻

▣ You're Standing in My Light ▣

"Paris," Bette Carsons was saying, "the city of light, the city of words. There we were on a barge on the Seine and everyone was saying, 'Shit. Shit. Shit.' "

The reason for the party was Allan Straight, in Winnetka on business. He had wandered into Bette's Books a month before to buy a copy of *A Moveable Feast*. "I've got a lonely night ahead," he said, "and suddenly I wanted to read about Paris." He had also said that he would be returning from San Francisco in a month, so Bette had invited Laurie and John Russell to meet him. Laurie had just published an article on Hemingway's Paris.

A fan whirred softly against the unexpected heat of the September evening. This was Bette's first dinner party since she had come home to Winnetka from California to live with Agnes, her mother. That was a year ago.

Bette continued, "The sewage of the Seine was going sssssh . . ."

Suddenly no one was listening.

Her mother was in the doorway, arms outstretched to greet them. Agnes's dress was blue—"Agnes blue" her many friends called this particular shade. Her slip was showing. There was a smear of lipstick on a front tooth and her mascara had already run down one cheek. She was shiningly beautiful. She said, "Bette, I told you it would be too hot for spaghetti."

Words flurried like birds before a storm. Agnes's eyes promised tales of wonder and delight, all the lovely adventures that had happened to her. Like Bette's, her hands danced with stories to tell.

"Cocktails?" Agnes said.

"Yes, Mother. I'll get you a V-8."

"But, Bette, I never serve alcohol."

"We're celebrating," Laurie said. "I sold an article to the *New York Times*."

Allan, sandy-haired, freckled like a boy, turned back to Bette. "And then what happened?"

Agnes took up the tale. "My daughter," she said, "had such a good time in Paris discussing dirty words."

Agnes told Bette's story well. Paris. Notre Dame warmed with lights in the dusk. On the barge, just off the Île de la Cité, Sterling Hayden and James Jones talking about bullshit. Bette saying at last, "Farmers find it useful."

Bette turned up the living room lights, went to the kitchen, and stirred the spaghetti sauce.

At dinner Agnes told about her days in Paris as a student. The supposedly strict chaperonage. The men who accosted her in the Louvre on Sunday afternoons. The night she and a fellow student dared go alone to a café after dinner. Then, in a half voice, as if to herself, as if bemused by the adventures she had never had, she said, "If anyone asked me now, I'd say, 'Do you have a heating pad?' "

Bette stared at her wine glass. Allan reached across the table and touched her hand. His pale eyebrows asked, "How come?" She shrugged.

"Ernest Hemingway . . . ," Bette said at last. Even the name did not sound right.

"Oh, that man," Agnes said. "Shocking. He spoiled Oak Park for me. I grew up in Oak Park. And all that about bulls and drinking day and night. Needing to box everyone. I do think literature should teach, should help. So few people understand."

"Mother, Laurie just sold an article about Hemingway."

"Really, Laurie? I'm proud of you. But I wish you'd come

to me. I remember what people said in Oak Park. It tells a lot, what people say. I sat next to Hemingway once at dinner, long, long ago, of course. I was very young and I went home and had a bath."

Laurie said, "Bette, let's have lunch Tuesday. I would like your opinion of my article."

"So few people understand," Agnes said.

Bette served coffee and dessert. Agnes said, "Cherry torte is really a mistake with spaghetti."

Bette took the wine from the table. In the kitchen she drank from the carafe. Allan came, carrying dishes. He said, "She turns out your light. Why do you let her?"

Bette did not answer. After ten years as an MIA widow, as Peter's presumed widow, coming home to Winnetka had seemed the right thing to do, sharing funds and expenses. After all, only she, among Agnes's four surviving children, was single. She had taken over her mother's equity in the big house and had paid the old bills. Now she saw the house as she had found it. Plaster flaking. Rugs stained. Empty bottles in the suite where a boarder stayed, his rent money supposedly helping to pay the fuel bills.

"Why, Bette?" Allan asked again.

She did not want to tell him that when she came home last Christmas, her mother had admitted to her that she had fallen twice and had lain all night on the bedroom floor, unable to reach the telephone.

She wanted to tell Allan that after Paris she had gone to Gstad. It was in Gstad that Yannick had come to her in a café and said, "I've been watching you. You're an immaculate bitch."

For a week they had skied and loved. Each day she had sent her mother a postcard. "Good skiing today." "The mountains are storm-bound. I spent the day, warm by the fire, with a friend."

When Bette came home for Christmas, Agnes had said,

"Margaret would have written letters. I suppose you were very busy." Sister Margaret had been dead for twenty-five years.

If only Bette could tell Allan about Yannick. It was one story her mother could never tell for her.

Instead she held the carafe and watched him watch her. "My mother had what she called her 'Gerry business,' " she said. "She took care of old people so their kids could have a vacation. She took them out for sodas and movies. Until she totaled her car in a ditch. She was seventy-nine."

Carefully he took the wine from her. She rested her forehead on his shoulder, and he lifted her head with a thumb. She kissed him.

"We should get acquainted," he said.

"Yes."

"Do you have children?"

"Lost one," she said. "I can't have any more."

"I have three," he said. "Sons. They stay with me every summer while their mother goes backpacking with her boyfriend."

"You're lucky."

"And I have a mother of my own. She's eighty."

"Do you live up to her expectations?"

He kissed her.

The next morning he sent roses, but he did not call. Bette did not plan another party.

As the days grew colder, Agnes spent more time resting on her bed. At dinner she frowned when Bette lit a cigarette and refilled her wine glass.

"I wish you wouldn't smoke," she said, batting the air with frail white hands. "And aren't you drinking too much?"

"I seldom smoke or drink except with you."

"Oh, Bette, my dear. I do hope you won't become alcohol dependent." And then, as always when she did not approve of Bette, she talked about Margaret.

"Margaret had such flair," she said. "I know Margaret would have been a great success. And she was so sensitive. Margaret always knew how to make everyone feel good."

"Maybe I should have been the one to die."

"Oh, Bette, I hate to hear you talk that way."

Each night Bette read in bed until midnight, slept until four, and then, awakened by an ache in her chest, made herself a strong bourbon and water and lighted a cigarette. One early dawn the doorbell rang. Two policemen whom she had known all her life were at the door.

"We saw your light."

"I read at four," she said. "I do a lot of reading for my shop." (Agnes called Bette's Books "cozy." What she meant was, "It's very small.")

After that, each dawn, the police tooted their horn softly as they passed. Bette flicked her light on-off in greeting.

Breakfast usually began this way:

Bette: "It's going to be a beautiful day."

Agnes: "The weatherman predicts rain and thunder."

Bette: "I won't be home for lunch. I'm going to meet Laurie."

Agnes: "I worry about Laurie. She drank three martinis that hot night you had the spaghetti party. And she couldn't keep her hands off her husband."

Bette: "After all these years."

Agnes: "Sometimes I just don't understand you."

At Christmas, her second Christmas with Agnes, Bette wrote her brothers. Tom who had a small orange grove in California and a wife Agnes thought not quite good enough for him. ("Though she does set a pretty table.") Anthony who sold insurance in Cleveland. James who taught Driver's Ed in Texas. Of her sons Agnes often said, "They could have done better," and "I don't understand why they drink so much when they come home."

Bette began her letter: "Just because I'm the baby of the family, a woman, and single . . ." She scratched out that sentence, tore up the page, and began again.

"I can't live with Mother any more. I can't keep up with the bills. She needs a cataract operation. She wants contact lenses. The fuel bills are exorbitant even though I've shut off the upstairs. (You may or may not remember that I turned the study into a bedroom for Mother, the maid's room into a very pretty one for me.) Mother needs the house at eighty degrees. The heat and the dollars flow up that great open stair she loves so."

Tom and James wrote. They had families of their own. School fees. Orthodontists. Insurance bills. Roofs that leaked. Anthony sent a check.

In January Bette found Agnes in her blue velvet robe lying on her bed as usual. Beside her was a small table she had brought from upstairs and on it was the crystal bell that long ago called a maid to clear the dishes and bring in the dessert.

Playfully Agnes tinkled the bell. The veins in her pale hands were blue cords. She said, "Now I can ring when I need you."

Bette found herself clutching the front of her mother's blue robe. She heard herself scream, "You do that, I'll kill you."

They both cried.

Agnes got up and made an omelet. She accepted a little wine with her dinner. They talked.

"Mother, sometimes you act as if you were jealous of me . . . any success, any happiness, any life I might still have."

"I have no reason to be jealous of you."

"That's what I mean, Mother. Can't you hear what you're saying?"

"I'm trying to speak the truth. I don't understand what's wrong."

"Mother, I'm trying to help us both live better. I keep pushing up. You keep pushing me down."

"I cannot help but feel," Agnes said, "that you are imagining things."

Three weeks later she fell and broke her hip. On the way to the hospital she told Bette, "I was trying to get dinner started for you."

The days grew gray. There was rain instead of snow. Each evening Bette went to the hospital. Each evening the nurses told her, "Your mother's our pet." "We've never seen such a sparkler." "She makes everyone feel good." "She brags on you and your bookstore all the time."

Home again, Agnes was brave about her walker. Agnes's friends came to Bette's Books and praised her mother's spirit and wit. What they were really saying was, "She shouldn't be alone."

Bette hired a woman to stay with Agnes. Agnes fired her. "You don't seem to understand," she said. "I don't want to dip into capital."

Bette's days at the bookstore lengthened into nights at her desk. She went over store accounts, house and doctor bills. When the police honked, she no longer flashed her light. Often in the morning she forgot to put on lipstick. One morning, she saw that her slip was showing and that her hair was streaked, mouse-gray. Sometimes in the evenings she forgot to shower. In the dim days of February, before going home to make Agnes's lunch, she would walk down to Lake Michigan to see the pale light on the water, consciously fighting the darkness that had taken over her life. She had long since given up her twice-weekly swim at the Y.

In May, there was a letter with a French stamp at her place at the dinner table. It was from Yannick.

"My daughter is going up for her *bac*. My eldest son is at PoliSci. My wife . . ." At the end he had written, "You lighted my life. *Je me souviens*."

"A letter?"

"From my French lover."

"Bette."

"He is. He was. It makes me happy hearing from him. He remembers too."

"You've gained weight. Are you pregnant?"

"Unfortunately, Mother, I've been here at home almost two years."

"You'll be punished for your sins."

Bette did not answer.

One more truth to accept. Peter's baby, lost so long ago. The hysterectomy. And her mother has forgotten.

Still, a lover, even a distant one, was a tonic. She lost weight. She bought a new suit. She felt her new skirt slide across her legs as she walked; the soft slipslide of her silk blouse caressed breasts grown tender with the spring. She moved faster, legs free, striding with remembered ease. She saw the world again. Old women who crouched as they walked. Lovers. She could feel the lovers touch. When she woke at four, she was trembling, moist, and ready.

Friends invited her to dinner once again. Men asked for dates. She said no. She knew what she would do if one of them touched her. She was not ready to risk her new gladness, not until she had made her decision about Agnes.

She could wait. She was only forty-three. Allan's business card with his San Francisco address was still in her wallet.

Laurie and John, her old friends from the spaghetti party,

showed her that the time for change had come. At a wedding reception, they were dancing. They moved far apart; their bodies twisted slowly. Laurie reached out to him and half smiled. John moved to her, and Bette, watching, felt a hot tenseness, then a sudden collapse, an ease within.

When she got home she found Agnes heating water for tea. The gas was high. There was no flame.

The next day she told her mother, "I'm selling the store and the house." (Allan's card was in her pocket.)

"My house, Bette."

"My house, Mother. Remember, I took title when I paid your debts. I've been adding and subtracting for months, trying to figure out what we must do."

"You're turning me out?"

"I can't be in two places, Mother. I want a home of my own again. I have to keep working. You need someone with you. I want to know you're safe."

"You're turning me out."

"I've been wanting to go back to California. We'll both go. A bookshop friend in Tiburon needs a partner. The climate will be good for you. With the money from the house we can afford a retirement home for you. There's a wonderful one right in Tiburon. With a view of the bay."

"I won't do it."

"You have no choice, Mother. I want to go and you can't afford not to. I can't let you stand in my light any more."

Agnes wrote her sons. Tom and James accused Bette of cruelty. Anthony had his accountant check the figures Bette sent him on the house and the investments she and Agnes shared. He flew in briefly, told Bette he would never speak to her again, and went home.

One of Agnes's friends sent Bette a letter from her mother. "This place is charming. The people, enchanting. Our kind. I've signed a life care contract. It's like going to college again, only the rooms are posh and the food is better.

There are classes and a book club. I can see the bay from my window. I wake each morning at three, turn on my heating pad, and watch a great gray eiderdown of fog roll back toward San Francisco." Scrawled across the top were the underlined words, "Good job, Bette."

In honor of her new life, Bette set up a dinner party for Allan and her Tiburon friends. In a month. When her new apartment would be ready. In the meantime, she treated herself to a vacation. She decided to learn to kayak.

As the kayak slid through gentle waters, Bette seemed to see her mother standing on a grassy bank. Her blue chiffon dress flowed about her slim body, still imperious, still beautiful. The glorious white hair, loosened by the wind, framed her face. Her slip sagged. Easy green hills rose behind her. If she were truly there, Bette knew her mother would be saying, "You're too old for this."

Bette waved at her instructor. She filled her lungs with the sweet-sour piney air, closed her eyes, and flipped the kayak into an underwater turn. For a moment of darkness she felt the water beat against her and she was sure she would never rise again. Then she came back into the light and skimmed past the now-empty hillock.

A week later she made her regular visit to her mother. Agnes was waiting for her. She sat with her face turned away. She did not speak. The room was dark. The heavy curtains were drawn. There was, Agnes had made sure of that, no view of the bay.

■

▢ **Triage** ▢

Peter is stirring the martinis, careful not to bruise the gin. Diane answers the telephone, hoping someone has the wrong number. On the telephone, Cliff's familiar twangy voice says, "Got a pile of straw in the basement for an old friend? How about adding some water to the soup?"

Peter downs his martini and puts away the bottles. Upstairs young Kevin and Andy are laughing. Kevin's acceptance from MIT came today, and Diane knows he is telling Andy just what he is going to do when, once and for all, he escapes the suburbs.

Half an hour later, Cliff comes in the open door without knocking, shouts, "Hi," as his host and hostess sit side by side reading the evening paper. His boney face shows surprise. "Give up drink?" he asks.

"Yeah," Peter says, his breath heavy with gin.

Cliff always calls when he is in town. He often invites himself to dinner, but he knows they have no proper bed for him. This time, with his usual candor, he explains, "Got thrown out of Tom's house. I set fire to my bed last night, and his girlfriend said I had to leave."

People their age do not have live-in girls. People their age do not set fire to their beds. People their age do not drop in and report, as Cliff had on his last visit, "The doc says the stuff's softened my brain," and then, coughing from emphysema, light a cigarette, and hold out a glass for a refill.

It is fifteen-year-old Andy—a study in freckles and charm—who asks Cliff about the dude ranch. "Hear old Kev fell off his horse the first day."

41

"Into a pile of ashes," Cliff says. "And where is my friend Kevin?"

"In bed," Diane says. "I was up all night with him. He's resting. Determined to get back to school and exams tomorrow. He'll want to see you after dinner."

"Came up blue and gray. June thought he'd died," Cliff says to Andy.

They are all remembering that Cliff and June had sent for Kevin last summer so that the only other dude Cliff had signed up would not be lonely. "Thanks for sending him," Cliff says.

"You're the one who offered him a scholarship," Diane says. "We've never thanked you enough."

They eat beef carbonade, a green salad, pears with an oozy camembert. Peter does not offer wine.

After dinner, Cliff goes upstairs and talks to Kevin, who is still weak from a night of vomiting. Diane hears laughter again as she washes each dish and places it in the dishwasher. She hears Kevin's voice rising and falling, saying, "Got myself a job at the drugstore to pay for riding lessons. Next time you're not going to look down and see me just lying there."

Later, as Kevin sleeps and Andy does his homework at the kitchen table, the three adults sit in the living room, their hands restless without a glass to hold. Peter is overweight in his carefully tailored striped suit. One of his feet tap-taps. His eyes focus somewhere beyond his old friend's right shoulder. He seems unable to speak. Cliff hunches over, a cigarette cupped backwards in his left hand, a habit learned on horseback. The gray tweed of his Harris jacket is loose over his shoulder. The jeans hang. The sole of one boot gapes. His tan has a greenish tinge.

The wind comes then, riding across the flatness of the land, whipping between the houses. Their oaks, newly trimmed, weave drunkenly. From the maple tree by the softly lighted terrace, the wren house swings and pitches. The Indian bells on the back porch sound a warning. Peter gets up and closes and locks the front door.

"What's doing, Peter?" Cliff asks at last.

"Tomorrow I get a renewal on the Natural Oats account and a vice-presidency. Or I lose it and get fired."

"Bad times," Cliff says.

"Win 'em all or get out," Peter says.

"Bad times," Cliff says again.

"Argentina taking over the Falklands," Diane says. "England rising up. 'Once more into the breach, dear friends, once more.' "

Neither man replies.

In the silence Peter's foot goes tap-tap.

Diane says, "Now that the English fleet is in the South Atlantic, will the Russians try to take over the North Sea oil fields?"

"Hardly Saint Crispin's Day," Cliff says.

Peter does not respond.

She tries again. "Even Einstein's in trouble . . . some astronomers in Arizona discovered a one percent error in his theory. It concerns the fluctuation . . . precession they call it . . . in the orbit of the planet Mercury. Anyone here understand that?"

Cliff smiles. Peter looks away.

Not so long ago, at Cliff and June's house in Libertyville, the two men used to set out, glasses and bottle in hand, Cliff beating the grass with a stick and saying, "Let's get away from the infantry," meaning Cliff and June's four girls and Peter and Diane's two boys. Cliff, six-foot-seven, Peter, shorter by half a foot. Both in jeans then, walking loose and at ease, genitals bulging. ("Don't talk to me about *Playboy*," June used to say. "I like to look at pictures of *men*.")

The two men would stay away for hours, discussing,

analyzing, matching wits and statistics. They both read compulsively, and they memorized arcane facts to surprise each other. In those days they talked about everything. Vietnam. The youth rebellion. Civilization and the barbarians within and without. Civil rights. Social legislation. John R. Commons. Marx. Compost piles.

"Crazy times," Cliff says now, drawing deep on his cigarette. His yellow-green eyes watch Diane. She wishes her hair did not look freshly cut and tinted. She wishes she had not gained five pounds. She wishes that, after her unsuccessful job interview, she had not kept on her new suit—ruffles at the wrists—so Peter could see it. She wishes the house did not look so neat and shiny.

"Nine percent unemployment," Peter says.

"Counting me," Cliff says. A half smile apologizes.

"Sorry."

Between each awkward phrase the wind beats on the large window. The trees groan and the branches squeak and twitter.

"Crucial age. Forty-three," Peter says.

"Turning point," Cliff says. "I remember."

"Kevin got accepted at MIT," Diane says into the silence. "Early decision."

"He told me," Cliff says. "We ought to be celebrating with champagne." The silence says, "What about my kids?"

Peter likes to say she talks too much. "Women," he often says, "don't understand the semantic pause. They interrupt before a man can finish a thought."

The semantic pause drags on. Diane says, "Excuse me," and goes to the kitchen, pretending there is work she must do. She puts the clean dishes in the cupboard. There is no sound from the living room. She reads a *New Yorker* story. Give them a chance to talk. Still no sound. At nine-thirty she returns to the living room.

Peter rises and shakes his old friend's hand. "Off to bed. Want to be fresh for tomorrow."

"Me too." Cliff's Adam's apple bobbles in a dry laugh.

At three o'clock Peter turns on the bedside lamp and reaches for his notes for tomorrow's conference. Diane has been awake too, listening to the wind that seems to toss the house like a small boat in rough seas. Through the unquiet night, trying not to disturb Peter, she has heard Kevin cough, then Cliff cough. She has waited for the smell of burning. Now she touches her husband's cheek— rough, needing the morning shave—and says, "Oooof," marital shorthand for "Heavy day tomorrow." She asks, "Would you like a massage? It would help you relax." Peter, his salt-and-pepper hair standing straight up from twisting and turning on his pillow, tries for a smile. It turns into a frown. "Thank you, dear. No."

From the next room she hears the scratch of another match, smells Cliff's cigarette, and trembles with the fatigue of two unsleeping nights. The bed seems to pitch and turn as if it were cresting a wave. Is Cliff drinking too, in that bed that is seven inches too short for him? Three times she has been sure his bed was burning. Uncounted times she has heard him stumble to the bathroom. Once, out of the darkness, Peter said, "Maybe after tomorrow we can buy a house where I won't have to hear the toilet flush all night."

"Oh, good," Cliff had said as she turned down the covers for him on the bunk bed in the study. "A bed light. Need that. I read a lot at night."

"Sorry it's so dinky."

The thought of their friend with no place to put his ankles and feet deepens her uneasiness. He is probably resting his head on one of the bookcases that enclose the bed. For the tenth time during the long night, she makes excuses. She could not have given Cliff one of the boys' beds. Kevin is still weak. Andy needs his sleep too. Glenbark High School does not rearrange exams because an old friend turns up unexpectedly.

In the old days, there were always plenty of beds and food and drinks at Cliff's winter cabin in Tryon. Cliff never counted his money—or anything—then. Peter had just begun in the advertising business. That was before Cliff lost the cabin and his business. That was before he and June sold their house and two cars and, three years ago, put a down payment on a ranch in Wyoming near Dinosaur National Park. June, as a girl, had spent her summers nearby on an uncle's ranch. Diane had visited several times. In her teens she had been the kind of girl mothers with sexually eager daughters invited to their summer places.

The ranch was going to make up for the lost family business. The ranch was going to salvage their marriage. ("I don't care about the women," June said. "Maybe they can help him. But not in my *house*." "It's June's fault," Cliff said. "She's always talking about my women and it makes the girls trembly.")

"Cliff's Castle," they called the ranch. Six thousand acres, if one counted up and down. Three thousand, level measure. The nearest town had a population of two. The ranch had its own electric generator and reservoir. It was thirty miles to the nearest commercial telephone, but a homemade telephone line on barbed wire linked it with a ranch across the mountain. The mail came once a week, if the carrier did not slide off the mountain road. Running cattle, hunters, and dudes meant a new life, Cliff and June said; and so, they set out for the west in a caravan—one ranch wagon and an old cattle truck, four daughters, one pregnant cat, two dogs, tomato plants and a seedling from a tree that once upon a time had been a seedling from an ancestral tree in Wales.

From the first, Peter had said, "There's no way they can pay the next installment." He had known all along that there was no money for cattle and that few dudes would forgo TV or relish a swim in the reservoir.

The bedroom is washed in pale amber light when she finally sleeps. Two hours later she is making breakfast for Peter and the boys. There is no sound from Cliff's room. No one at the round cherry table in the kitchen talks. The boys peer at her as if through a fog. They too have had a waiting night. The eggs are soggy. The toast is like wet paper. The coffee tastes as if she had not scrubbed the pot. Each time she brings fresh toast or jam to the table, she touches Peter's shoulder, waiting for him to speak. He is rereading his presentation. When he does speak, it is to say, "I wish Cliff would get up."

After breakfast, Kevin sits, shaking his head as if to fight for the clarity he will need today. Peter puts his arm around him, holds him for a long moment. "You'll do fine," he says.

At the front door Peter says, "You've got to get Cliff out of here. Tell him to go. I wish I could stay and do the dirty work."

"Our friend," she says.

"Our life."

(June had said on the telephone eight months before, "I've left him and moved to Casper. The doctor said I was doing all the wrong things. Making him feel comfortable in idleness. If he gets going again, tries to work, he can come stay with me.")

Diane watches her men cross the lawn to the car. The wind wraps Peter's tan raincoat around his legs, and billows the boys' red jackets. Kevin, pale but determined, walks beside Andy. Small branches and half-budded twigs lie on the lawn. A large limb has fallen across the front fence, crushing the emerging tulips. "Don't let him burn us out," Andy shouts as he gets into the car. Kevin punches his arm. It is not a playful blow.

Cliff comes down at ten. There is a tremor in his fingers. She serves him sausage and three eggs, English muffins and marmalade. There is a fresh pot of coffee. When he lights a cigarette, she reaches over and takes one from his pack. "Shouldn't," she says.

"No," he says and leans back in the straight wooden chair and stretches his legs across most of the kitchen. She turns her chair and holds her jeaned legs out beside his.

"You're a little one," he says.

"But rugged," she says. "Tell about the ranch."

"Lost it."

"The good parts." She has written publicity pamphlets for Cliff's Castle and fed news items to the local press. "DUDE FALLS INTO DINOSAUR FOOTPRINTS" was one head-line. Three times she invited friends to see Cliff's slides. Three times guests thanked her for the party and did not mention the ranch.

"More coffee?" she asks, and then, "I talked to June. She loves teaching." ("I gave the ranch a good try. We lived on the deer we just happened to run into with the ranch wagon off season. I got drunk so I could let him touch me.")

"The kids are in school in Casper," he said.

No more drives for June across the rough forty-five miles to the district school. No more staying overnight in a cabin when the roads snowed over. No more getting up in the icy dawn to relight the wood stove. ("I wait until I have a hot flash," June wrote.) Diane wishes she knew how to say to Cliff, "She will raise strong daughters."

"How's your neighbor across the mountain? June's tele-phone pal?"

"Eighty-two and still riding cows."

The neighbor had made a good publicity item. While Cliff was back in the Midwest corralling dudes, the rancher used to call June each evening on their private telephone. Once, in a spring blizzard, when Cliff had just come back to the ranch, the telephone rang and a voice said, "June?"

"Nope. Sorry. You must have the wrong number," Cliff had said and hung up.

Diane tried to place that story in the *Junior League News;* it turned out that June had dropped out years before.

Because she cannot think of another question, Diane says, "Let's take our coffee into the living room," and then, "Let me mend your jacket."

The lining hangs below the hem. The silk has torn away from the seams.

"You'll be glad to know I have another one," he says.

"I am."

He used to order shoes from England. She remembers the absurdly elegant morning coat he wore the day he married June in the big house near the lake in Winnetka. He bumped his head on the chandelier as he went to her. Everyone laughed, and Cliff said, "Whoops," and grinned his incandescent grin.

Now he tells her stories about the ranch. (Had he cared that Peter did not even ask?) He makes the failures funny. As he talks she is going over the budget for the year, reviewing the bank balance in the hope, which does not make sense, that she can come up with a figure that will justify paying for Kevin's summer at the ranch.

They are not smoking so much now. They are both laughing, as the tales of disaster and broken hopes pile one on another. She is sure now that Cliff must stay until he finds a job, a home. If Peter does not finish his conference today and needs sleep, he can go to a motel. She is sure Peter will understand until, at noon, the mail comes. Real estate bill. $1,234.67. Peter reminded her just yesterday that it was coming. "The smallest, oldest house in a good neighborhood" is the way she always describes their house. There is also a letter from MIT for Kevin. No, it's for Andy. Next year Andy will choose his college. A letter from her mother that will surely beg for a visit and add, "I'm sorry we can't send airfare this time." An insurance bill. "The great invisibles," Peter calls these expenses.

She puts the rest of the mail aside without looking at the envelopes. She hands Cliff his mended coat. "More coffee?"

"No thanks. Out with it. What did Peter tell you to tell me?"

"That you have to go."

"Yes."

"Lunch first?"

"Just ate. Remember?"

"That was three hours ago. We've been talking like kids."

He smiles.

"Do you have a place to stay?"

"One night. Yes."

He stands at the door, his duffel at his feet, hands on his hips, a remembered gesture of ease. He bends over her. "Thanks, little one. Good memories."

"I'm sorry."

His fist touches her chin. Dammit. He still gets the girls trembly and he knows it. Once, years ago, she had stepped back quickly from him, saying, "June's my best friend." She wonders if June knew.

"It's now or never for Peter," she says.

"Lighten the boat."

"Sorry."

"Stop saying you're sorry. Peter needs his sleep. At forty-three and all."

She goes with him to his battered ranch wagon. "Well, good luck."

"Why not? Lady Luck's my best buddy." The gravel of the drive splatters as he drives away.

———

She spends the afternoon picking up small branches and twigs. The limb is wedged into the fence, and she cannot move it.

Peter's face is mushy with fatigue when he drives in from the station. He does not kiss her. He says, "Nothing settled, but there's still hope."

She does not answer and he puts down his briefcase and comes and holds her close. His hands rub her arms, up, down. "We're still afloat," he says, and then, "I didn't want you to have to do it."

"Never again," she says, stiff to his touch.

She wishes she could believe it.

◻

◼ Goodbye, Charlie ◼

The house I grew up in fronts a ravine. Throughout the seasons the ravine changes from flower-spangled green to deeper green, to orange, red, and brown, then cools to black on white; and all through my childhood, no matter the season, at five-thirty each afternoon, a woman's voice called from the opposite side, "CHARLIE . . . CHARLIE."

When I was ten, tall for my age even then, with skinny black braids tickling my back, and too many bones, I said to my mother, "When I grow up I'm going to marry Charlie."

"Why not?" Mother asked.

We never met, Charlie and I. Any bright spring day, I could have gone down the ravine and climbed to his door, but I was a shy girl.

Through the years, coming home less and less because there was no longer a place there for me, I would ask, "How's Charlie?"

"He seems to have grown up and moved away," Mother would answer in mock surprise.

Last August I paid my parents a visit before the fall term at Goddard, where I teach. This time I had a mission: to help Dad and Mother. Then too, I was hoping to tell them how I was.

I took the limousine to Highland Park. "Your father hasn't been driving lately," Mother had written. She has never learned to drive and I suppose she thought that once Dad took late retirement, he would drive her everywhere and it would be like the days of their courtship, only better because now they had money.

Dad was in his pajamas in the living room by the big window to the ravine. Head down. Shining white hair uncombed. Hands loose. "Honey baby," he said. He was drunk.

Mother was in her Lilly Pulitzer candy-sweet greens and pinks. She looked stunning, as always—tall, as we all are, big-boned, and thin. Her tawny hair was blunt-cut in the manner of the athlete she never was. She moved slowly, measuring each step.

Dad looked me over as if he were considering hiring me. "Is that what professors wear these days? Jeans? All that hanging hair? I believe the proper comment is 'Far out.' "

"Not really. On campus I'm thought of as conservative." I was wearing all my gold chains, long earrings, and an asymmetrical resale-shop Bill Blass top in deep shades of green. Silently I noted, "Defensive." That is my procedure for utilizing anger.

"When I was in high school," Mother said, "my mother made a fuss because I went to Union Station without a hat."

"*Plus ça change . . .*," I said.

If I were to do a case study of Dad, I would describe him this way: *Handsome still. Square Germanic face. Scar on left cheek from a jagged tin can. 1931.* (Mother encourages her friends to think it is a dueling scar.) He smelled of booze. It was four-thirty in the afternoon.

Dad said, "There's a gray streak in your hair."

"About time. I'm thirty-nine."

"Tea?" Mother asked.

"Nonsense," Dad said. "A drink."

"I don't drink any more," I said.

My room still has acres of flounced organdy. The strawberry pink walls are newly painted. A collection of foreign dolls fills a bookcase. Mother still saves them for the child she is sure I will have.

Bob, my only brother, has already fathered five. "Good genes," Dad likes to say about Bob's children. Just the same, last Christmas, he said, "I don't want those kids here until they learn discipline."

"Smart going," I said to Bob when he told me about his appointment to the University of Hawaii. "That's where the job is, f'rgodsake," he said, but he knew what I meant.

Dad has another favorite saying: "Homosexuality is nature's way of killing off bad genes."

Beside my bed was the picture Dad took when I was a junior in high school. One shoulder is bare. My head tilts unnaturally. I remember Dad saying, "Look at me over your shoulder. Smile." On the back of the photograph he wrote, "Daddy's girl."

That spring I threw the picture, silver frame and all, against the living room wall and as the glass splinters fell on Mother's pearl gray carpet, walked out with the guy I was dating. I did not come back for three days. Did Dad remember that when I came home he stepped back as if I had the plague?

I pressed my forehead against the window that faces the ravine. It was sun-hot. "Hi, Charlie," I said. "Be happy. I am." I repeated a lesson from my Alanon days: "Adversity provides the opportunity to practice maintaining your own serenity."

The heavy solemnity of this good advice always amuses me.

I telephoned Ellie back in Vermont. "I can't wait to tell them about us," I said.

She said, "Spare the old folks."

Dinner was whitefish with shrimp sauce. Barely cooked beans with dill. Baked potatoes. Salad with Grey Poupon vinaigrette. Mother had lighted the candles. Hair still rumpled, Dad was in his Bean corduroys and a plaid shirt. He was drinking a martini.

"So," I said, "what's with retirement? How do you feel about it?"

"I don't." He got up and made another drink.

"There's lots to do out there, Dad. People need your skills."

"You're an expert?"

"That's what I teach, Dad. The psychology of aging. Sex after seventy. How to . . ."

"Helluva subject. Spare me."

Mother's knee nudged mine under the table.

"So what are you doing?" I asked.

"The plant moved to Buffalo Grove. I went out there a few times."

"Every day," Mother whispered, kicking me. I ignored her.

"And?"

He did not answer.

"So how does it feel?"

"They don't want me there."

I put my hand on his.

He pushed my hand away.

"Well, thank you, dear, for the good dinner." He had not touched his food. He took his half-filled drink to the sideboard. When he came back, it was half-full again. He kissed Mother on the cheek and went upstairs.

I called from the bottom step. "Dad, let's talk."

He slammed his door.

In the dining room, Mother was staring at the candles. "Teresa, must you?"

"I want you and Dad to tell me about you. I want to tell you about me."

"You can see how it is."

"But the house looks beautiful, Mother."

"The decorator just left."

"I thought Dad was going to do it."

"Well . . ."

"You're tougher than I thought."

"I didn't want you to feel sorry for me."

"I'm going to write you up. For *Psychology Now*. I have a contract. Autonomy. No matter what."

She said, "Not really," but she was pleased.

The next day I found the car had a flat tire. I called the garage. Later I took Mother shopping. "What have you been doing?"

"I walk to the village. I order by telephone."

"Moooooother." I sounded like an adolescent again.

"Friends pick me up for meetings. For lunches. They always have. I volunteer at the hospital. I need to get out and work with people. Happy people."

I gave her a hug of praise.

Tuesday, I took her to lunch at the Art Institute. Afterwards, we wandered, seeing again the Calder Flamingo. ("I still want to push it back," she said.) The Nevelson. ("I know it's chic to admire the El behind it, but it's too fussy for the sculpture.") The Chagall wall. ("So sentimental. Isn't it wonderful with the harsh tall buildings? And remember Chagall kissing Mayor Daley?") The Miro. ("She reminds me of Mayor Byrne.") I drove home the slow way so she could see Michigan Avenue and the Outer Drive. She cried out her delight like a child. Then, suddenly, she slept.

That night, Dad and I talked until midnight. Rather, he talked, telling me again the old, old stories.

"Well, Ph.D.," he said, "at least you didn't have to drop out of school in the fourth grade."

Dad sold newspapers, then victrolas, to support his mother and two sisters in Kansas. In 1933 he rode the rails to Chicago.

"I switched to radios," he was saying, as if I had never

heard the stories before. "I had just saved my first nickel and along came the war."

"Still hear from your Seabee buddies?"

"Damn right."

He told me again how he worked his way up the hierarchy at Elite TV, going to night school year after year on the GI Bill. When he wasn't at the plant or at school, he was painting the house, adding the cantilevered deck over the ravine. When he ran out of things to paint, repair, or build, he chopped down trees, raised prize roses, and made fine cabinets. Once in a while he would go to a party to please my mother, and halfway through the evening she would find him on the telephone, maybe to France or Japan, telling a colleague about a project he had worked out during dinner.

(Last week I told Ellie about pushing Dad into his first and last father-daughter Scout baseball game. "He didn't know what a bat was for." I love telling Ellie family stories.)

"We did it, baby," Dad was saying. "We beat the Depression. We won the war. We rebuilt Japan and Europe and didn't drop the bomb again. We did it and no one gives us credit. All you Ph.D.'s . . ."

"Yes?"

"We thought we'd whipped the Japs fair and square, once and for all, and then they took forty percent of my business. No one knows what we did. You Ph.D.'s in flimflam. You babies in fancy jeans. GODDAMMITTOHELL." His huge arm crashed on the table. His beer bounced to the carpet. Amber liquid spilled before I could retrieve the bottle.

"GODDAMMIT. GODDAMMIT."

"Yes," I said.

"That shirt you're wearing. Where'd it come from? Hong Kong?"

"Yes, Dad."

"Everybody's buying foreign and then you women, you

women insisting on jobs, causing unemployment."

I said, "Let's go out and kick a tree."

The next morning, Wednesday, Dad was dressed by eleven. His hair was combed. He made burgers for lunch on the deck. His voice did not slur. There was a small glass beside the grill, handy, I thought, for dousing flames, until I tasted it. Vodka.

I kept Dad talking all afternoon. Soon, soon, I could tell him my news.

Thursday morning I drove across town for a surprise visit to Gwen, my long-ago best friend and one-time matron of honor. She was not home. I sat in the car and contemplated the white slatted fence covered with morning glories, the pseudo-Georgian pillars, and the three bikes in the garage. Did the children have her mustard-blond hair? Blue eyes? Little round calves? Did they smell of apples and grape bubble gum?

Home earlier than I expected, I found Mother on her knees by her bed. She was not praying; she was changing the sheets. There were tears in her eyes, more from my finding her so than from pain.

"Mooooooother," I said again. The teen in me seemed to have returned to stay.

"Eleanor Roosevelt turned her mattress every week until she was seventy-five. All my life I wanted to do what she did."

"Like the Declaration of Human Rights?"

"Yes." She wiped away a tear. "My mother always called her 'That woman. That immoral woman.' "

"She was a great lady."

Neither of us thought I was referring to my grandmother.

"You remember John Brinker," Mother said. "He's in Tucson. He can hardly stand. Can't move his arms."

John Brinker. A giant like Dad. Ten years older. Strong

and dark. He retired early to play golf, ride, and swim most of the day, then to drink and eat hugely and talk in an excited shout most of the night. Still unassuaged, he would read until dawn. Once upon a time.

"John went riding the other day," she was saying. "He got the idea it would loosen him up. He was lifted, strapped on. He made the horse canter. Then again, again . . ."

Her voice faltered. "John rode an hour. The next day, the stable man refused to let him take a horse."

I was beside her now on the floor, holding her gingerly, not sure how much touching hurt her.

"Scared?" I asked.

"Shitless." I had never before heard my mother swear.

"What are you doing about it?"

"Exercise. I get out when I can. Laugh. Hug." She hesitated. "But not so much as I pretended. When I come home, your father acts like a young bride. Neglected."

"Most brides don't drink."

"Teresa."

"It's in the books, Mother. Even mine."

"Mostly I'm just here. He depends on me. He always has—for everything but his work. He stands behind me when I open the refrigerator. He says, 'What are you going to do with that lemon?' "

I held her closer. "One thing I want you to know, I want you to know that any time you can come and visit me." I did not have to wonder if Ellie would approve.

"He tells me how to pre-spot his pants. He doesn't like the way I load the dishwasher. He shows me how to endorse a check. He wakes me from my nap, holding out a cup, saying, 'Someone broke it.' "

That night I treated Mother and Dad to a rib dinner at an old-time favorite restaurant in Highwood. I did not order drinks. Nor did Dad. He kept the waiter busy refilling his water glass. He told old war stories. Mother and

I laughed and nodded. He emptied his plate and reached over to Mother's for more. I said, "Dad, we still haven't decided what you're going to do with your life."

"Don't Ph.D. me," he said, but he was laughing.

Friday I filled the car with groceries, and when I came home Mother was on the telephone saying, "She still calls herself a radical feminist, whatever that means."

I said, "You know what it means." She probably did not hear. I did not repeat. She had enough to deal with.

In the afternoon, Dad and I walked down into the ravine. Good memories came. Spring beauties. Violets. Trillium. May baskets and bouquets for favorite teachers. The fort Gwen and I dug into the hill. Our bouncing tree. We would climb to the top, hold tight, and jump until the tree swayed. It was like flying. Hanging from a low branch, we giggled because our groins throbbed.

Dad's step was firmer. His cheeks were flushed, but it was from the heat. We sat side by side. He said, "You never did marry Charlie."

"Never did."

"Too many Charlies."

"Not really, Dad."

Neither of us was going to mention the one I did marry. Sweetheart roses banked high in the warm brown oak elegance of the Episcopal church. ("The religion of butlers," Dad liked to say.) Gwen in sapphire chiffon. Four bridesmaids. A reception and dinner at Exmoor for one-hundred-and-fifty. Mother's best friend gave me a set of twelve Lenox service plates. "I got three sets," Mother said.

"His hands are too soft," Dad used to say of my husband, but he and Mother were eager to see me safely married. ("And not thinking so much," one of their friends said.) Six months later, his degree from Harvard earned, my husband decided we should build a Buckminster Fuller dome on a Colorado mountaintop. Seek truth in sacred mushrooms and muscatel. "Everyone expects too much of us after Sputnik," my husband said. I am glad I do not have to be twenty-four again.

"Any more Charlies?" Dad was asking.

"No, Dad, but I'm happy. I'm a good teacher. I have this really good friend. We're renovating a barn. Ellie's older than I and . . ."

"Glad to hear it, and now if you'll excuse me."

"Dad, I'd like to tell you . . ."

"Dearie," he said, "I'd better lie down before we start for the airport."

Watching him toil up the steep ravine, remembering the trembling fingers, I did not call him back.

Mother and Dad were waiting in the car out front. I went through the back door and out on the deck, the long-ago picture in my hand. "Well, Ellie," I said to the ravine, "I'm on my way home." I swung the oval photograph as if it were a Frisbee, imagining how it would sail over the ravine, dip, rise, then fall, lost forever, no longer a token of the way my parents wanted me to be, lost in the bramble of blackberry bushes and pine. Then Dad gave the old-time beep-ba-beep on the horn, and I slipped the picture in my purse. Ellie would want to see it.

□

◾ Cooked ◾

Half-past seven. The telephone rings. I pour my first cup of coffee, straighten my backbone as I was taught, and reach for the telephone. (My grandmother, who had the first telephone in Plum, Kansas, always took off her apron before she touched the receiver.) Ceil, my older sister, my only sister, is calling. *She* always smiles as she answers the telephone, but she is widowed now, as I am, and her smile is a relict of gentility.

"I didn't sleep all night." Ceil's voice lifts as if she were announcing, "We have good news today. Our speaker is . . ." These days the lilt of her voice runs counter to her words.

I am trying a new method with her: rough love. At first, after her husband's death, I sympathized, but then I decided sympathy is debilitating.

I say, "So get dressed. Get to your job."

"I can't. I'm sick."

"You'll feel better if you go out."

I have this theory that Ceil should work—something to put on a pretty dress for. That is simple of me. Even in the kitchen she wears spike-heeled designer shoes and soft long-sleeved silk dresses. I usually wear clogs, a smock, and the Peruvian silver pin my husband, Don, bought for me in 1974.

"You and *work*. Work isn't everything."

I say, "Mmmmmm," and prop the telephone on my shoulder. As I sip my coffee, she lists her sorrows: No sleep. No friends. No money. People working against her.

Loneliness. The Midwest. Her all-white condominium on Lake Michigan.

Most of her complaints have no reality.

"I should never have come back when Richard died."

I reach for my toast and breathe in the sweetness of strawberry jam. I chew. I repeat, "Mmmmmmm?"

"I have to see you today."

"Not today." Coffee spills on my tawny handwoven cloth.

"I'm lonely."

Ceil has dinner with friends three or four times a week. Her three kids call every Sunday from California. Mine seldom write or call, but the six of us—five now Don is gone—always meet somewhere for Christmas.

I say, "Today we have a presentation to get out by three. I can't talk today."

I live in the loft above my late husband's studio. He was stripping the brick and installing plumbing when he died. One large room holds his paintings, not the advertising work he did to survive, but the real ones. I hung a dozen of his oils for the celebration of life party I gave instead of a memorial and sold two paintings as his friends sipped the commemoratory wine.

For a while, after Don died, Barbara whom he trained and Caroline our so-called office manager and I made do with leftover sketches. Now we are on our own.

As for the apartment, there are old timbers in the high ceiling. My trestle table and Shaker chairs stand against the mellow brick. Shaggy weeds in copper washbasins fill empty corners. There is a working fireplace. In the spring my living room and bathroom windows look out on the flowering branches of an old apple tree.

The Northwestern trains run right by. (Mother used to say, "Nothing is more important than a good address.") I wear earplugs at night; yet often I lie awake as engine-lights sweep over me and the old timbers shimmy and shake. Even the bricks try for a small dance, but they are too solid for more than a shiver. I am still only five minutes from Lake Michigan. A spiral stairway takes me down to work each morning.

"I'm due downstairs in seven minutes." I interrupt Ceil at last. "We're finishing a presentation for Apex Air."

I usually do not explain business to Ceil. Richard never told her about money or taxes or insurance or bills. Now, however, rough love seems to demand more explanation. "We sent a presentation to Young and Fort last week. It got lost. If we don't have a replacement in by three-thirty today, we're cooked."

I just reread *A Farewell to Arms* and am enamored of the word "cooked." Ceil and I were gently bred, as the saying went in Evanston years ago—meaning unseemly problems and words were never expressed—so when I read Hemingway in college, his soldiers sounded almost genteel. Even rereading, I wondered about soldiers cooking— in a pot?—until I said the word aloud.

Now, trying to make Ceil realize how it is with me, I mention our accountant. (Ceil detests the word; Don would laugh to know we have one.) "Our accountant," I say, "tells me that if this presentation doesn't go, we're cooked. Cooked, Ceil. *Fini.*

"We have until three to finish. Barbara will deliver it. Tomorrow I give an oral presentation."

Ceil says, "Please come today."

"I'll call you tomorrow evening." I hang up.

When Don died, the kids and I and three couples from our apartment building sat around the dining room table, Don's paintings like ikons on the wall, all of us saying, "Ceil's coming."

That meant, "She'll know what to do." She always did until Richard died.

At sixty Ceil has pale peach hair, twisted up and up, elegantly. I'm fifty-five. My hair is always falling in my eyes, but it looks as if I had paid seventy-five dollars to have it frosted.

She is tall and she sweeps through a room like Lynn Fontanne. She likes to say she has Dad's hips (large) and Mother's breasts (small). I have never known Ceil to envy me anything but my figure, which is nothing more than trim. I cannot see how she can envy me. She is a woman of transcendent beauty; and yet, when her friends speak of her, it is always her tenderness they remember. In all her life I have known Ceil to do only one unkind act and that was for me. My fifth-grade teacher stuck chewing gum on my nose. Ceil sent her a Shalimar bottle filled with urine.

"She probably douses herself with it every morning," Ceil said.

Ceil has hundreds of dear, dear friends. I have five. She is always flying across the country to solace the sick and the dying. I am afraid I might meddle. She sold a large house in Massachusetts when she came back to the Midwest. For thirty years Don and I shared a sunny apartment near the University Club. When it turned condo, I moved here. She met her Richard at a Harvard mixer; he inherited old money. I had known Don since fourth grade; for thirty years we played musical chairs with bill collectors.

Downstairs, my young friends and I—relics of the Don Anderson Art Works—sit around a drawing table, pasting up. Barbara wears size five skinny jeans and a white Save the Whales T-shirt. Her skin is black satin. Her ebony hair falls squarely to her waist. Her nose is of astonishing straightness. Caroline is softly blonde. She will have dumpling cheeks by the time she is my age.

The telephone rings. I hold a drawing between thumb and forefinger. "Barb, please answer."

A frown crinkles Barbara's Queen Hatshepsut nose. "It's Ceil."

"Please take a message. I'll call later." The drawing in my hand twists on the page. I pull it up and place it properly.

Barb says, "Ceil wants you to come to dinner."

"Not today."

"She says it's important."

I feel the hook go in. I wait for the tug on the line.

"She says she needs you."

A train passes. The table rocks. I jerk back. A pot of rubber cement overturns.

"She says six o'clock."

"O.K. Sometime. Whenever I can make it. Sometime. Around six."

Barb slams down the phone. "She kept saying six."

"How did she sound?"

Barbara's lips twist with something that might be sympathy or scorn. "Cheerful, as always."

(Mother liked to say, "A lady's voice is *sunny*. Always.")

Caroline's eyes cut to Barb who gives a slight nod. I am not sure what they are saying. Younger women understand people better than I.

I try to understand how my sister has changed. Just before Christmas, I went to see her doctor. "What can I do to help?"

He said, "She feels abandoned," and patted my hand.

"Nonsense. Eighty-seven of her nearest and dearest friends live in the Chicago area. Two of them took her to England last fall, just after her husband died."

I stopped. Did my envy show? Richard asked me to go with them to Paris once. Going would have hurt Don. Richard—no one ever called him Rick or Dick—was one of the few people Don disliked. "An elegant, arrogant Yahoo," he used to say.

"Just treat her as a friend," Ceil's doctor was saying.

"Have dinner with her two or three times a week."

"I don't have dinner with anyone three times a week. I'm a working woman. Most evenings I go to bed with a book."

"She needs you." The doctor patted my hand again.

"I know Ceil worries about things that aren't—no money, no friends—but she's always cheerful."

I could not give my worry a name. ("Hug your troubles" was Mother's final solution.) I tried. "Ceil will never talk about what really hurts."

The doctor tapped his prescription pad as if he might write one for me. "That's the problem," he said.

I did not tell him that for the first time in our lives Ceil and I had almost quarreled.

"You're not even unhappy," Ceil had said. "And Don's only been dead three years."

"Don doesn't want me to be unhappy," I said. "I'm too busy to brood." I was not going to say, "except at night." Ceil and I had already had that discussion. "Oh, you and *sex*," she had said.

I am still wondering why, that time she spoke of sex, she added, "Damn you."

One o'clock. Two pages to go. The page I dumped cement on cleaned up well. The old school clock on the wall clicks off the minutes. Every half hour the building shakes as a train passes.

At two I answer the telephone. It is Ceil. "You will be here at six?"

"Ceil, I can't talk now."

"You never can when I need you."

"Not today." I might have said, "Today's hysteria day," only that is not what I am feeling. As we paste and paste, I see that Barbara has done a good job. The Don Anderson Art Works will survive. Nor do I want to tell this beloved sister that I feel more competent when I stay away from her.

She says, "You don't give me comfort."

"Write down your troubles. Figure out what you can do about them—one by one."

"Oh, do. You always want me to *do* something." Her next words are, "I made chocolate mousse."

"I'll be there," I say. "Sometime."

"Sometime," Caroline repeats and drops her scissors. The points graze her hand. Blood spurts, spotting the cover page beneath the title. I mask it with an ink swirl which may or may not be my initials.

Minute by minute the clock on the wall urges us on. Long ago, while Ceil and I were visiting our grandparents in Kansas, a sudden wind by the wheat field caught me, and pushed me with the same pulsating power. I had been listening to the crickets call, remembering Grandfather telling me that once upon a time the prairie grasses grew taller than he. Then from the cobalt sky there came such a wind that cattle moaned and chickens screeched. I saw Ceil coming to find me. I ran toward her. The air smelled like a burnt-out fuse. Suddenly I was hurtled into her arms; and as we fell together, she screamed. I laughed.

At two-thirty Barbara goes upstairs to dress. Caroline and I reread the text, forward twice, then from the last word to the first to make sure once again there are no typos. My stomach tilts. One foot is twisting, left-right, left-right. I do not want to see Ceil. Not today.

At five minutes to three, Barb comes down dressed for her client call: charcoal suit, crimson blouse, the requisite soft tie, spiked pumps. She has braided her hair and turned it under like the clubbed tail of a race horse and placed a red rose in the dark shining coils. Under half-moon brows, electric blue eyeshadow and a wide white line mock the tailored suit. I push back my bangs and wish that just once I could look like that.

Side by side, amid the smells of coffee, rubber cement,

and Barb's funky perfume, Caroline and I present our finished work. Caroline makes a mock trumpet salute with cupped hands: Ta-ta-ta-ta. I say, "We're not easy to cook."

Barb says, "I'm going to celebrate with a drink on Rush Street after. If nothing happens there, I'll go to a movie." Her dark eyes appraise me. "Why not come meet me?"

"Maybe tomorrow. After my client call."

We both know neither of us will ever enter a singles bar.

Caroline goes home to make dinner for her husband. I clean the studio and climb the stairs slowly, complacent as a cat. It does not occur to me that someone else might win the Apex account.

Bliss is lying in the deep, brown-tiled tub admiring the handthrown bowl and the copper soap dish a friend designed for me. Through the high window I see apple blossoms. Bees swarm in a pulsating haze of gold, white, and black. Barbara used a branch from this tree against a silver plane for the first Apex Air pictorial.

I say to Don, somewhere off in the world, a leaf blowing in the wind, a tick in some fundamentalist's short hair, "You'd be proud." I push aside a new thought: five larger agencies are competing with us for this account.

Still, the tiredness comes, the loneliness, the need to hear Don's voice again. I sink deeper, letting the hot water ease me. One of these days I will learn to lean over that table without hurting my back. The water ripples around me. The five-thirty-nine passing? The five-fifty-one? I am so weary I do not hear the rumble-screech of the train. Even the telephone is silent. I unplugged it when I came upstairs.

I must have slept, bathed in quiet warmth and the scent of lemon bathsalts Don loved. By the time I am out of the tub, my hair still moist, dressed in my favorite dirndle, and on my way to Ceil's, it is six-thirty. Still I remember to plug in the telephone. It rings when I am halfway down the stair. I do not go back.

The elevator to Ceil's top floor apartment clicks and hums. I am looking forward to a double Scotch and my first cigarette of the week. It will be like old times. I will say, "Did a good job today," and Ceil will say, "You'll win this one."

I knock on her door. There is no answer. So much for Ceil and her insistence on six o'clock. Beyond the door a telephone rings. Rings. I pause for a second, waiting. Still it rings. A dear friend saying, "Dinner Friday?" "Join us for the symphony?" "Goodman Theatre?" Still the telephone rings. I knock harder. I beat the wood. A chill wind seems to blow down the bright corridor. Sweat slides down my inner thighs. Still the ringing. Ringing. I shout, "Dammit, Ceil. Let me in." Dread scratches my throat. She takes too many pills. There are knives in the kitchen. I will not scream. No matter what lies beyond the door, I will not scream.

I rummage in my purse for my key to her apartment. I drop the key. The key sticks in the lock. I try again. I push with my knee. The door opens at last. She is beside the great window to the lake, the faint bloodied reflection of the sunset on the water beyond. By some trick of light—is it the sunset reflected on the water, on the window?—she seems outside, beyond the glass. Slowly, out there beyond the glass, she turns to me. She is wearing her best blue silk dress. Her makeup is perfect. Her hair has been done in a new and dazzling style. Her needlepoint lies in her lap. She says, "You're very late. What if I really needed you?"

▣ A Certain Difficulty in Being ▣

Every afternoon, ever since Harrison died, as the clock in Bea's bedroom sounded four, John Dickerson ("Doctor John" as her children used to call him) telephoned. One hundred and ninety-two times, his voice still rough as burlap, saying, "Beatrice? Beatrice, dear?" One hundred and ninety-two times, reading in bed, mourning her life, she had hung up. Until two days ago, when she put down the Simone de Beauvoir she was reading—a map of Paris beside her on the bed—ready at last to answer his call.

Now, his hand over hers, John leads the way, past pale chintzes and soft anonymous faces. (Her glasses are in her purse.) Beyond the round damask-covered tables, a low fire leaps. Between them the air trembles.

Does he stoop a little? She feels taller with him now.

He pulls off her white gloves. She says, "How did you know I was longing to eat at Le Provençal?"

"I used to call you Frenchy." His hand moves lightly up one finger, down, then up.

"A long time ago."

"You're beautiful, Bea." His voice trembles. "You said, 'Look for Whistler's Mother.' "

"I got fancied up." Her hair is newly silvered. Her wedding pearls and red dinner suit light her face just as she planned.

"We don't change," he says.

His hair is longer and gray, but he still wears a proper charcoal-striped suit with a heavy red knit scarf. His front tooth still tilts. He still smells of spices and touches her hand each time he speaks.

"We've changed," she says. "So many lives. Vietnam. Recessions. Reagan. Death. Harrison's death."

"Anne's death," John says. "Seven years ago. Within the week every hostess in Delray Beach had a house guest, maidens and widows all. Not one had forgotten to oil her lamp for me. What are you drinking these days?"

"The same. Champagne."

Cases of Piper Heidsieck had been Harrison's sole patrimony—champagne and the tall Victorian house, the only shabby one for blocks, with motes of pale paint forever floating from old mullians and flakes of plaster in her saucepans.

John's words tumble over hers. "Tell me everything."

"You first," she says.

All she knows about him now is that he has come north to take her back to Florida. That he has a big pink house on the ocean and a clinic in town. "I do the thinking. Younger doctors do the work," he had explained on the telephone.

He places a plane ticket on the table. "You'll want to check out my house, my finances, my friends. Health. Disposition in the mornings. The sun will do you good."

He has forgotten. She has avoided sun and sand ever since her last child could bicycle to the beach.

"John, I'm used to making the plans."

"Please, Bea. We don't have much time."

Through the years she had introduced a carefully prepared plan with, "Harrison, you used to tell me . . ." Sometimes it had been easier to say, "Yes, Harrison . . ." and then do exactly as she knew she must. She says, "John, you used to say . . ."

"I'll think for both of us. Just for a little time." Then quickly, (Is she frowning?) "As the kids say, 'Your place or mine?' "

"Too fast," she says, but she laughs.

"Last time you said you were married and had four small children, a remark lacking your usual wit."

Even her daughter will not believe she is hearing thunder among the chintzes. Her sons, no doubt, will merely shrug. They remember how she used to explain to strangers at a cocktail party why no matter what she did she got pregnant. They remember their father saying, "Tact in audacity consists in knowing how far to go too far." Any good family friend knew he was quoting Cocteau who was quoting Péguey.

Harrison had another saying: "A good marriage begets remarriage." Her sons, she was sure, would say, "It sure would help pay the bills."

It had been a long time since she fell in love with John. She had fallen in love because Harrison did not want to leave the house after his bankruptcy. She had fallen in love because John made saving the baby's life seem easy.

She slips the plane ticket into her purse. "Forget Whistler's mother," she says. "Look for Ninon de Lenclos."

She has forgotten Florida. Sun, sand, and Maxfield Parrish sunsets. Filet mignon. Potatoes baked in foil. Lemon pie with eight-inch meringue. Shrimp, shrimp, and more shrimp. No need to go to the kitchen or pick up a mop.

John wants her with him all the time. He shows her his clinic. He leads her through his great pink stucco cube of a house, demonstrates the filtering system for the pool, and explains the composition of the clay tennis court. He shows her flippers, masks, golf clubs, rods, reels, tennis rackets, cameras, tripods, and light meters. He buys her a BMW.

He kisses her awake each morning to swim, to sun, or ocean fish. (She refuses to play golf or tennis ever again.) Her walking, her swimming, and her lovemaking have a new lightness. Her nails grow and she lacquers them pale peach.

Sometimes, close to him, listening to the waves come and go beneath their window, she thinks of reading late by the fire with Harrison and of the sweet solace of a shared champagne after a day of pretending bankruptcy was fun. She turns to John to forget.

John's friend Dottie invites them to brunch by her pool. Braless, in a copper-bright and almost topless sundress that matches her tan, she wears stoplight red lipstick. Her wrinkles look planned. She says, "Welcome, lovebirds."

The other guests seem to have wandered in from another party. Three women wear short-sleeved linen dresses with intricate embroidery insets. (Bea has already learned that the most expensive dresses in town are extra large on top.) The men are deep-bellied in plaid or jade or white slacks. There is no Mr. Dottie.

"John has good taste," Dottie says, noting Bea's raw silk slacks and shirt, a gift from John. (At home she wears jeans and Harrison's old shirts.)

Blue Linen says, "Maybe now John will settle down."

"A cute lady," Plaid Slacks says. (Bea deplores both words.)

Dottie says, "John, we've been waiting for you to explain this new bag lady Medicaid fraud."

The men retreat to the end of the patio and talk about the Dow Jones, Jade Slacks's stroke on the tenth, and their children—ages thirty to fifty.

Yellow Linen says, "Do you have children, Bea?"

Blue Linen says, "John says you're from Evanston."

Yellow Linen says, "Elsie's pregnant again. The doctor . . ."

"Your son-in-law should . . ."

"My grandson said . . ."

"My great-grandson said . . ."

"The man at Peacock's looked at my diamond and he said . . ."

"Bea, dear, your pearls are beautiful."

"Thank you." ("They are all I have and I'll walk in sackcloth before I tell what the Tiffany's man told Harrison: Small but perfect.")

Blue Linen: "I bid seven spades and she bid . . ."

Dottie: "I want to ask John what to do with my Caterpillar stock."

Yellow Linen: "We wouldn't have any fun without Dottie."

Lavender Linen: "My husband calls her an LOL."

Blue Linen: "Lecherous old lady."

Yellow Linen: "I do hope you'll marry John."

Bea: "I already feel married."

All through the "days of dollars and shits" (Harrison's phrase), her friends used to invite her to hear Adrienne Rich, to see Martha Graham, to picket the South African consulate, or attend an Alliance Française gala, and she would answer, "But I can't leave Harrison alone with our six fish, one of which is very small."

Here there are brunches, early poolside dinners, greyhound races, jai alai matches, and games at the Royal Palm Polo Grounds.

At home, Bea would lean across the table to Harrison and, in the breathless tones of one of her Great Books members ("my Big Bookies") discussing "Plato's odd notion of love," repeat a confidential conversation:

"I never thought MY marriage would break up over SOCKS. I said to my husband, 'If a brilliant lawyer like YOU can't match his own SOCKS . . .' "

One of these days she will mimic Dottie. One of these days she will tell John why she does not laugh at jokes about ERA, Gerry Ferraro, or the woman who decided she had not been raped after all.

Sometimes at the Florida parties she wonders why she does not go home; then John touches her.

One Sunday he takes her to church—a handsome miscegenation of airplane hangar and flying saucer. "All those months I was calling you," he says, "I was looking for a church you'd like."

Where hangar and saucer meet is a rock pulpit. She whispers, "Upon this rock I found my church?" The sun through a round skylight haloes the minister's bald head. At the base of the rock, in a mass of flowers, a spider spins her web. John strokes her hand and she almost forgets the morning papers: He marked all atrocities attributed to the Nicaraguan government; she underlined those thought to have been perpetrated by the rebels.

After the service John introduces her to the minister. "Tim Allardyce, my bride-to-be. Tim and I have talked about a May wedding."

"But, John . . ."

"I've ordered a wall of orchids."

"Then Africa?" Tim asks. "In June?"

"Africa? But John . . ."

"I've signed up the best hunter in Nairobi."

She can feel and smell it now: *Exit Beatrice Webb. Enter Memsahib Dickerson. Limping. Khaki culottes. A pith helmet.* She says, "Osa Johnson took rose-patterned buttermolds on her first safari."

"We'll learn Swahili. A beautiful language, Bea."

"Shall we learn just the imperative?"

He does not understand.

"John, what does one talk about in Swahili? Please, I don't want to go to Africa yet. I haven't been to Paris for forty years. I've read everything. Memorized maps."

"I've always dreamed of Africa with you."

"Paris first, John. I know everyone there. Racine. Diderot. Voltaire. De Beauvoir. Harrison felt the same way."

He stops her with a kiss.

In January John gives yet another brunch at his club. Bea checks the buffet table. Surrounding an ice swan are slices of pineapple, mango, kiwi, strawberries so perfect they might be wax, and blueberries like small plums. A salmon swims a sea of lox and avocado. There are three kinds of quiche and a mountain of shrimp.

(Back home she gave candlelit dinners; flickering lights threw camouflage patterns on frayed damask and spaces where once had stood heirlooms beyond her repair. The invitations in her finishing school backhand read, "Dinner at seven. Baked beans and champagne." At home she made laundry and weeding and canning peaches from the back yard so amusing that the neighborhood children begged to help.)

Dottie comes to fill her plate with strawberries. Her tiny hands dance to the beat of a calypso band. She smiles as if they shared a secret. Bea begins, "John told me . . ." She wants to ask about the son who went to Canada, the son Dottie has not seen since.

Dottie says, "Did John tell you about his heart attack? I feel I should." Her voice slithers down an octave. "You see, I worry because he was with me."

Bea holds out her glass to a waiter to be refilled. "Thank you, Dottie," she says. "I do need to know, don't I?"

Dottie moves back to John, hands on hips, her feet barely moving. John does not touch her but their steps match. When the music stops, John kisses her cheek and goes back to talking about unemployment behind the wall in the black section. "My father was a janitor during the Great Depression," he concludes. "I made it anyway."

"Notwithstanding," Bea says. No one looks at her. (Harrison would have known that the word was Nietzsche's.) She raises her half-empty glass. "To Martin Luther King. He would have been fifty-six today."

The silence is like a gunshot.

The sigh of the waves lull her. John's fingers stroke and enter. She says, "Not tonight."

"Close your eyes," he says. Gently he ties her hands to the bedposts.

She stiffens, turns her head away, says no. His lips skim her body, probe and tease until she rises and falls to his touch, crying yes.

She sleeps quickly, then within the hour wakes. Waves whisper and hum as she seeks a word to describe the difference between Harrison's love and John's. (Find-the-word was one of Harrison's favorite games.) John has helped her love again. (She: "My pond's turned to dust." He: "That's what you think.") Harrison made love with her. John makes love to her.

When he wakes her the next morning, she groans. "I've been waiting," he says. "I don't like to eat alone."

"Too early." Her body aches from the night. She burrows into the pillows to shut out the calypso he pipes through every room, wanting only to spread out across the bed and sleep alone.

Fifteen minutes later he is beside her with a breakfast tray for two. After breakfast he shows her the latest arrivals from Abercrombie and Fitch: khaki culottes, a tent, a double sleeping bag. She tries on the culottes. "Cute," he says. The khaki scratches.

At eleven he takes her down to the beach. The sun sparkles in a royal blue sky, but the palm trees rattle and screech against a swift wind. Beneath a lime-and-tangerine umbrella she watches him plunge into the heavy surf. She blows sand from her book and straightens her glasses. She is rereading *Candide*. Sand swirls around her bare feet. John is beyond the waves now, swimming strongly. She brushes sand from her cheek and closes her eyes.

Sand blowing. Leopards coughing. Camels sobbing. Elephants uprooting trees for breakfast. The stench of a lion's breath in their honeymoon tent. Sand in their sleeping bag. John in the sand, his face blue. Dottie dances toward her to a calypso beat. She shakes down a thermometer. Trailing Dottie is a parade of urinals, bedpans, and an oxygen tent.

She knows what is happening to her: an epiphany. The heavens have not opened. Angel choirs do not sing. Her epiphany is more like biting into a soda biscuit after a piece of double chocolate cake, and she knows that never again, day or night, can she say another false yes. She opens her eyes.

John rises on a swell, waves, then rides the breakers. At the ocean's edge, he straightens stiffly and slips a pill from the packet on his belt. She wants to run to him, to hold him close, to say, "We'll both change. We'll both learn to give a little." Instead she walks slowly back toward the house.

He comes to her on the terrace by the swimming pool. "Why didn't you wait for me?"

"I had to think."

"No one else thinks so much."

Her hand is over his. "Dottie told me about your heart attack."

"When the day comes we'll go out in a small boat in a storm and make love."

"I don't want to die at sea."

"What's really bothering you?"

"A certain difficulty in being." Harrison would have known she was quoting Fontenelle.

John says, "What?"

"I don't want to spend the rest of my life competing with the Dotties."

"They'll miss me."

The difficult part is done. "And there's so much else I want to do."

"You'll miss me."

"Maybe Harrison spoiled me."

"Yes, for me. I'd still like visitation rights. Once a year?"

She does not dare touch him. She says, "Why not?" and lets him be the first to walk away.

■ The Long Homecoming ■

Steve Lathrop was sitting stiff-backed and naked on the hard bunk when his wife came into the cell to get him. Louise still wore her white uniform under her tan raincoat. The acrid prison smell of disinfectant mingled with her perfume. Tweed. If only she would wear the Muguet de Bois he had brought from Nam. And the bright scarf.

Sweat coursed her cheeks like gray tears. The pupils of her eyes seemed swollen, too large to see him. Usually, in her uniform, she put on a brisk nurse's air, but now she was like a child just waking. He wished he could take her in his arms and comfort her, but she had come too soon. He was not ready for her grieving.

"The officers were kind, very kind, Steve." Louise was breathing fast. "They came to the hospital and drove me to pick up Stevie at school so I could take him to Aunt Jane's for the night and then to the apartment for your clothes." She dabbed at her nose with a kleenex. Her hair lay dank across her forehead.

His throat was too dry to say, "I'm sorry." He held tightly to the clothing folded in his lap.

Louise seemed to see him for the first time. "Did they strip you?"

"I undressed," he said.

She stood, suitcase in hand, looking down at him. He wanted to cry out to her, "Scratch out my eyes. Do something." Then perhaps he could explain.

Instead, the soft whiteness of her throat tightened as she tilted her head to the left, then up, her signal, always, that she was going to be brave. She folded the tissue in half, in quarters, then again, and put it in her purse. She placed the suitcase on the clean tiled floor and knelt and opened it. The sighing sound of her breathing was loud in the silent cell. Without a word she handed him gray slacks, a white shirt, brown shoes, and socks and a necktie. His glasses. The raincoat that matched hers.

Heavily, slowly, he gave her the pink silk dress, the girdle with the pink satin bow, the high-heeled white patent leather shoes, the matching purse, and the Christmas wig Louise would never try on. Their fingers touched. Hers were so cold that he shivered.

She held the pink dress against her breast and waited for him to speak. All he could think of was how she would look in the dress. She had the body for it. Small-boned, seemingly fragile like his mother. Louise did not have to wear a cincher to have a waist. Nor pads for breasts and hips. Nor another pad to make the dress fall smoothly in front.

Louise had everything. The right to shop day after day for powders and perfumes and dresses. The right to wear pretty, soft things. He had hoped that having Stevie would round her out a little. That now that he was home from Nam she would wear more makeup and curl her hair.

Louise said, "I'm taking him home, Officer."

The desk sergeant signed Steve out in her custody. "Straighten up," he said. "You've got a good wife."

Steve felt his wife's hand tighten on his. He had had to promise to go to the University Health Center, but somehow he must tell her that he had waited six months for today and that he had no wish to be robbed of it ever . . .

He had felt the nylons touch and slide, touch and slide as he slowly went down the steep stairs. The risers were so shallow that even in his army boots he had to walk sideways. Never in his long planning for this day had he thought to practice going down in high heels.

He had hurried on tiptoe through the newly painted front hall that was warm with the crusty cinnamon smell of cookies baking. He closed the front door quickly.

Outside in the late afternoon brightness, the last of the geraniums flamed against the green of clipped privet. The sun glinted on brass knockers on doors painted red, blue, orange. The tang of the flowers and of newly raked leaves sharpened the sweetish smell of pot that seeped through the tightly closed shutters next door. The thin eerie sounds of a Hindu raga were like the caress of a fingernail down his spine.

The straps of the bra were firm on his shoulders, the girdle, delightfully tight, the skin of his newly shaved thighs, soft from the long soak in the big old-fashioned tub. Everything was too bright, too intense. He had never smoked anything, but this must be the way his men had felt as they smoked pot and watched the tracers from their guns rain unending streamers of red and green fire in the gray dawn.

He opened his eyes just in time to keep from walking into a woman. Fat. A bag of basketballs tied together with a belt. The long belt-ends swayed menacingly as she walked. Her ankles were surprisingly slim. Louise would never have worn such dagger heels. He almost ran back to the apartment. Would the woman laugh at him? Call the police? Perhaps she would take off one of her shoes and strike him.

Then he saw that her thin eyes looked deep inside at something that displeased her and suddenly he *wanted* her to look at him. He held the purse tightly with both hands to keep from touching her arm and forcing her to see him. He needed to have her look, to know that in his ruffled dress and despite his almost six feet of muscle and bone, he looked more of a woman than she. And still, as the stir of his body told him, male.

At the corner he stumbled on a high uneven curb. He

looked back. The woman did not turn. Anyone could stumble. Louise often did because she did not look where she was going. She said it was because her mother called her clumsy.

He touched the mailbox at the corner with white-gloved fingers and was sorry he had promised himself to go no further. His head no longer ached as it had for weeks, his chest no longer cramped. He let the handbag swing and his hips sway; he clicked the high heels on the pavement. The quicker movement heightened the scent of his perfume. He breathed deeply, trying to describe it: Lily of the Valley. Sugared tea. Musk. The cool murmur of the taffeta slip made him feel . . . complete.

A yellow car passed, each part meshing, turning. One spark plug missed. Somewhere, down the block, children played. Their voices were as fresh and distinct as if they romped by his side.

He neared the apartment. His landlady was on the porch under the flag that flew rain or shine. Broom in hand, she peered down the street as if she were looking for a child or a dog. But she had neither. Usually, at this time of afternoon, she was in her kitchen, her voice, exactly one quarter note flat, sirening old hymns through the house. Now he would have to go around the block.

When he got back to the corner, Mrs. Barton still stood, austere, impassive, watching the street with a frown that made a V sign on her forehead. He went around the block again. Then again, this time more slowly. The mail-order pumps cut into his instep. The purse grew heavy. Surely the bell on the woman's stove would call her in soon.

Louise and Mrs. Barton always talked about plants. Louise loved to explain that plants grow better if you talk to them. Or, if you have to go to work, leave lights on and music playing. When Louise was working, he and Mrs. Barton talked about Nam.

Louise called Nam "dirty business, man's business."

Mrs. Barton thought he should have come home to ticker tape and parades.

Maybe if he walked right up to her, Mrs. Barton would invite him into her warm bright kitchen and talk about pork roasts and feather stitching and her new fall coat. Today he did not want to talk about Nam.

Yet he had only done what had to be done. Shot a lot of Gooks. Monday, Wednesday, and Friday, North Viets. Tuesday and Thursday, South Viets. Given the kids chewing gum and candy and money and never once gone with the sisters they offered. Gotten dysentery and a sliver of land mine in his shoulder. Back home, in the hospital, he had first thought about the nylons the nurses wore and wondered how they must feel against their skin.

The sun was setting, staining the sky red. His legs ached from toes to groin. He could not walk another step. He turned toward his door and the pain in his thighs was like salt, sharpening his pleasure as he faced Mrs. Barton.

"Help you?" His landlady's words trailed away in doubt.

He stood for a moment smiling at his friend. Her frown deepened and she worried a graying curl. He stepped back and shook his head as if to say, "Wrong house," and retreated. Tears stung his eyes like sweat.

Halfway down the block, he saw a child sitting on a low brick wall. She was holding an empty cone in her hand and sobbing. The ice cream lay at her feet. He eased himself beside her, skirts prim across his knees. Like his long-cherished heroines-at-home in the old war movies—Greer Garson, Claudette Colbert—he clasped his hands to one side and slipped off the left pump.

The child wore a ruffled sunsuit and smelled of clover talcum and vanilla ice cream. Her freckled legs were patched with bandages and a front tooth was chipped. She looked about five, just Stevie's age.

"When I was little," he began as he often did with Stevie.

She was crying too hard to hear how once he had dropped his ice cream and turned and run back to the drugstore to demand a refill. And had gotten it. His mother never tired of telling that story.

"You can do it too," he said.

The child sniffled, gulped, and stopped crying. She shook her head.

He said, "If you really want something, you have to get it for yourself."

She rubbed her hand across the tears and dirt and ice cream on her chin. "You walk funny," she said.

"My foot hurts. Joan Crawford says it's crude to say, 'My feet hurt.' "

She moved closer and touched his skirt. "Pretty," she said. The warmth of her body eased the ache in his legs. She looked up and patted his cheek, and he knew the contentment Louise must feel when she gathered up one of the stray cats or dogs or broken-winged birds she was always bringing home; when at bedtime she held Stevie, snug in his Doctor Denton's, and read to him about Peter Rabbit. Serene. Necessary. Whole at last.

The child's sticky hand slid down his cheek. "You've got a funny face. Too much goo." She rubbed the makeup he had spread to hide the roughness above the dress. Then she screamed, the high cutting cry of a police siren.

He was almost home when a car pulled up beside him. There was no siren. The policeman at the wheel said, "Get in." They rode in silence. The sergeant at the desk booked him for disorderly conduct. "You're lucky the mother don't want to get you on molesting a child," he said.

Louise held tight to his hand as they stepped out of the police station into the neon glare of College Street. Slowly, in their dun-colored raincoats, they pushed through the swirl of embroidered jeans and fatigues emblazoned with upside-down flags and infantry patches. The lights dimmed as they walked beyond the crowd, turned into a quieter street, and, still clinging, hand in hand, turned again at their corner and came to the steep stairs to Mrs. Barton's house and their apartment. The necktie around Steve's neck was like a noose.

In their bedroom Louise slowly and with a calm that frightened him swept his makeup bottles and tubes into the wastebasket. She gathered up the dress from the suitcase and sat at his desk. He heard the soft sounds of silk tearing. Wordlessly, still in shock, she picked up the big desk shears under his study lamp. Before she could begin to cut, he was on his knees, hands spread to protect the dress. He did not let himself cry out. Instead, he forced himself to speak in everyday tones. "I'll give it away in the morning, Lu. No need to waste it."

She pushed him away and stood and threw the dress into the corner by their brass bed. He reached out to her and she drew back, screaming, "How could you? How could you?" When he could not answer, she came to him and rested her head on his chest and now her voice was a low cry. "But why you, Steve? Why you?" Then even more softly she said, "You've always been so strong. That's why I learned to be strong while you were away."

The words he chose to explain did not reach her, but she listened, trying to understand his hurt. Hours later, in the big bed, his head on her breasts, she was still questioning, questioning, trying to comprehend and to console him.

"I remember the dress," she said at last. "We saw it last week in Penney's window and you wanted me to buy it and I said it was too ruffly, kind of too much, maybe. You seemed so disappointed and I wondered about it. But, Steve, it's just too, well, too pretty-sweet. And then you bought it."

"I need it," he said. "I always will."

In the dark she stiffened against him, yet forced herself not to move away. "You're the only person I've ever loved," she said. "I didn't think it would turn out this way."

Slowly he shifted his body until she lay against him, her head on his shoulder, and when she said, "My mother always says I'm not woman enough for a real man," he answered, "You're woman enough."

Only then did she weep beyond comfort. "It was that child, that child in Vietnam."

The child. Nothing but the eyes above the peeling flesh still lived. He could not help her, but he sat in the mud and stroked her hair.

"Maybe," he said.

Somehow, he felt, the story must be older, much older, but he did not want to go back now. He reached into the corner by the bed for the pink dress and let it whisper through his fingers until the stir of his body told him he was ready. He slipped on the gown and quieted Louise the best way he knew. Her nails dug into his shoulder. She cried out three times.

"I truly, truly don't understand, but I'm going to try," she said as she rolled away. "Just so no one else ever knows."

She slept and as she slept he saw again his men beside the dun rice fields, under the rockets. Then, even more clearly, he saw himself. He was standing with Louise in a crowd of women before a table heaped with multicolored scarves. He was wearing the pink ruffled dress. He reached out and touched the shining stuffs and the colors—smoky sharp—seemed to spin and eddy under his hand, faster, faster, brighter, brighter. He had to close his eyes at last, but the soft streamers of silk caressed his trembling fingers and he was reconciled.

Louise stirred and sighed. Slowly the dream faded. The ribbons slipped away, and he knew that for the two of them that which was most difficult in his long homecoming would begin when she awoke.

■

◼ To the Sacred Dark ◼

Vincent, my mother, was by the fire in her bleached jeans when I got home from visiting Grams at Sunrise Skilled Care. Mother's hair was down; her white uniform was already in the washer. She was smoking a joint, the first in five years as far as I know. She's on a health trip—jogging and saving her chromosomes—in case she ever has another kid.

I try not to think about that. Making babies is messy, and even though Mother doesn't look her thirty-eight, she hasn't much baby time left.

She's like a kid herself—dark hair parted in the middle, a redness on her high round cheeks. She makes me feel outsized, but Grams used to say, "Elisabeth, you're not big, just too old. Vincent tells you too much."

Now Mother held out a letter. It was from Roland Folsom, a lawyer, setting up an appointment to discuss child support. For me.

We had talked about this for months. (Mother tells everyone, "Elisabeth's my good friend.") It wasn't until we began to discuss paternity payments that I realized that before, except when I was two, she did most of the talking. Then she would decide what to do and I would say, "Yes."

Mother often mentions the year I was two and she was in nursing school. "Two is a negative phase," she says.

"From the terrible twos to the terrible teens," I said last month.

She let out a yell. "No." We held each other and yelled together because we had this big problem.

Now I threw the lawyer's letter at the fire. It slid off the firescreen and fell at Mother's bare feet. "I won't go," I said.

"You have to."

"You chose to have me. You told me so. To have someone to love you. Always."

"True. I was a dumb kid. Now I'm responsible for you. And for your grandmother. Her rent just went up."

"I prefer not to think about that."

"You 'n' me."

"Whom do I claim as my father? Do I tell about the men who stay over? How you keep your diaphragm airing on the top of the toilet? Do I explain to the lawyer about filling in questionnaires the first day of school? Name, address, sex, birthday, father's name. Does the lawyer know that now Grandfather's gone I just X-out that space? That my father's name is X? Do I tell him that Grandmother's neighbor used to smooth her white gloves, put on a sweet look, and whisper, 'Bastard,' as I went by? About Parents' Night and my friends' mothers and dads saying, 'And where is your father tonight?' "

Most people don't know that because of the commune my name is Elisabeth Starlight Reeves. Sometimes my mother tells them. I wish she wouldn't.

"We claim your father. Jacob."

"Jacob didn't want to be my father. He just got you pregnant. You told me."

"Jacob was the one."

"Then why doesn't he come see me?"

Mother pretended not to hear. "He promised to help you. Always. He wanted to. I didn't want him to until now. I hear he's inherited money."

"Yuck."

"Yes." She closed her eyes the way she does when she is holding back. "Why don't we run this conversation through again in twenty years and you're a mother and see how it comes out?"

That was when she began to call me "Judge."

She had told me about Jacob and the midnight covenant many times. Why she dropped out of Iowa State her freshman year. Why she and her friends went west to think. ("To fuck," I said. Mother always says that word as if it were honey. She's a romantic. What can I expect? Her parents named her after their favorite poet.)

I understand how it was. The war. The guilt. Eating and sleeping and dressing, clean and regular, while across the world mothers and kids starved and flamed up like torches and died; but I'd been reading about mothers and kids in Ethiopia, in South Africa, Cambodia, Angola, in San Salvador, and I wanted to say, "It couldn't have helped those kids much, your going to Colorado to smoke pot."

The day she felt me kick, she walked up the mountain to a religious commune. She wanted to live clean and good again for me. ("You're my miracle baby.") The religious people talked about gentle Jesus and caring and ate only vegetables. Then the Big Man, their leader, switched to the Old Testament and sin. Mother's sin.

My mother still doesn't know how Grandfather figured out what was happening, how he found her, but one day he and Grandmother drove up in a Jeep. Big Man wouldn't let them in. His disciples gathered around my mother. They chanted, "Devildevildevil."

Grandfather and Grandmother saw that I was almost ready to be born and that their only daughter's arms were black and blue. They came back the next week with a team and kidnapped Mother. They took her to a motel, locked the doors, and closed the blinds. They took turns talking to her for five days and five nights. In June 1972, my mother went home with my grandparents to the big stone house in Evanston. When I was ten months old she began her nurse's training.

"A bad time," I said to Grams years later.

"Yes, Vincent cooked everything with herbs and brown rice."

Money is one of the things my mother always prefers not to think about. (She went to college with seventeen cashmere sweaters from Peck and Peck.) It was not until Grandfather had been in the hospital six months that she discovered he had used his clients' insurance payments to pay for her kidnapping. ("I'd do anything for Vincent," he said.) His theft was settled out of court.

Mother is still paying his debts. When he died, she sold the big house and we moved into this one. We kept Grandmother's best furniture. Grams said, "The fireplace must have been made by a master mason," and then, just before this disease got her, "I never thought I'd live next door to a garage-door factory." I slept in a closed-in porch until Mother sent Grams to the nursing home because she kept wandering off, looking for Evanston and Grandfather.

"I must tell Stan," she would say. "They've bombed Guernica."

Our appointment with the lawyer was for December sixth. Nothing seemed to go right as we waited.

I promised to stand straight, to answer questions in my friendly voice, and not to comb my hair when the lawyer was speaking. Mother didn't believe me.

She was reading a blue-white-red-on-gray book called *Handbook on Child Support Enforcement*. She had sent for it from the Natural Child Support Enforcement Reference Center in Rockville, Maryland.

"Natural?" I said. "Better than bastard."

She almost slapped me.

"We could go on welfare."

Then she did.

I tried to cheer her up at dinner with a story I'd learned at Grandmother's Bible class.

"Did Big Man at the spook commune tell you about Sarah? Old Sarah was listening at the tent door and she heard the Lord say to her husband, who was ninety-nine years old, 'Sarah, thy wife, shall bear a son.' Sarah hadn't menstruated for maybe fifty years and so she laughed within herself and . . ."

"Judge," my mother said, "if there is one thing I can't endure right now it's for you to get religious."

After she had underlined most of the sentences in the *Handbook,* she got out a pile of photographs and showed me my father. Jacob looked like a moulting stork.

"He's got money now," she said, "but he's going deaf. Rock music."

"He doesn't look very clean."

"Hitchhiking was not conducive to cleanliness."

The next day I threw up in English class.

Friday I announced at dinner, "I just discovered some geese are monogamous."

"Judge, just shut up."

(Mother used to say, "My parents are the last monogamous couple in the U.S. of A.")

I worked at the supermarket Saturday and Sunday. On Wednesday, as usual, I visited Grams. (The other afternoons she plays Bingo; Mother calls Bingo "Nursing Home Valium.") On the way home I threw a roll of toilet paper into the tallest pine in Bittsie's yard.

Bittsie is my best friend. Or was. She says she is going to be a famous artist, but I don't see how, not now that she has a boyfriend and giggles and squeaks all the time. She practices eye contact and tilts her head. "A courting signal," she calls it. She reads jail-bait magazines where the girls lie around making eye contact and wait to be raped.

(Before she got this disease, Grams told me, "Women's

magazines are sexist. I don't want you wasting your eye-sight reading how to be popular.")

That day in cafeteria Bittsie told me she and her boy-friend french all the time. "We've made an early New Year's resolution," she said. "We're going to Planned Parenthood together."

Bittsie called during dinner. She told Mother about the toilet-papering and she cried.

Mother said, "Elisabeth, why?"

"I can't stand it, her getting a diaphragm."

"Judge, you and I talked about this. We must take care of our bodies ourselves. If Bittsie is going to have sex—and I agree she's too young—she must take care of herself. That her young man wants to go with her is a positive sign."

"Yuck."

"Would you rather she got pregnant?"

"She could wait until she's famous. Then she wouldn't have time."

Mother said, "How come you're growing up a prig?"

I threw up in geometry class. I was sure I had AIDS or Herpes and that I was tall because Mother had done drugs.

"Mescaline," she said once, "is good for meditation."

I said, "What did you meditate about?"

I threw up in study hall and the teacher sent me home.

I didn't have a fever on Friday, so Mother insisted I go with her to the lawyer.

Mr. Folsom's office had furniture like Grandmother's. On his desk a white wooden ibis stood on one leg and looked at me. Copper scales held incoming and outgoing mail. He wore a pink shirt. His blue blazer had silver buttons. Only a jogger could wear his slacks. I hoped that now Jacob had money he looked like Mr. Folsom.

Mother had put blue on her eyelids and red on her cheeks. Her hair was braided in tight buns over her ears.

She looked like the wooden doll Grams gave me for my fifth birthday.

Mr. Folsom wrote down Jacob's full name: Jacob Andrews Abelson. His address and telephone number in New Hampshire. He asked Mother how she knew Jacob was my father. (I didn't listen.) He explained ways and means of getting Jacob to support me: wage withholding, automatic bills, property attachment, tax refund offset, garnishment, liens.

"Jail," Mr. Folsom said, "would be our last option. And now, I must ask you again. Are you sure Jacob Andrews Abelson is the father?"

"Yes." Mother's voice was iron. She gave the lawyer Jacob's picture.

"We hope that once your situation is explained to him he will agree to monthly payments so we will not have to go to court. Should he not so agree, we will have to order blood tests to prove paternity."

I inched my chair closer to the copper bucket he used as a wastebasket. I might need it.

"These tests," he was saying, "must be administered before the child is eighteen. These tests exclude ninety-five percent of men wrongly accused." Holding Jacob's photograph as if it had Herpes, he dropped it in a folder.

"Now," he said, "you say all the members of this Starlight Commune swore to take care of this child? Why?"

"I had the baby for everyone."

"Do you have anything in writing?"

"It was midnight." Mother's voice trailed sweet and frail, as if she had been smoking again. "We sat around the fire. It was cold, very cold, and there were stars. We wrapped ourselves in blankets and huddled close. We reached out and held each other's hands, one on top of another, all intertwined, all the hands, all the lives, all the reasons not to be part of the death world back home, and we agreed that Jacob and I should have the miracle of a baby for the commune. We swore, each of us, we swore to the sacred dark that we would support and guide this child forever.

"I did not touch another man until I was sure I was with Jacob's child."

"I see," Mr. Folsom said. Then he said, "Well," and pulled the information about Jacob from the file again. "I shall send a deputy to find this Mr. Abelson."

"Yuck," I said.

I had decided not to vomit. As usual the grownups were being impractical. I said, "What I'd do is call Jacob right now."

They turned to me as if they had forgotten I was the reason for this meeting.

"With Mr. Folsom as witness," I said.

"Yes," my mother said.

"Now." Mr. Folsom handed Mother the telephone.

Jacob answered right away. The rock must really have gotten his ears. He shouted as if he didn't need a telephone just from New Hampshire.

"Money for Elisabeth?"

"We swore. Remember? I can't do it alone any longer."

He said, "I've ordered this new Jeep . . ."

"Give me the phone," I said. "Hi, Dad."

"Watch it," he said.

He did not hang up; the telephone did not buzz. "Jacob," I said, "I didn't want to rush you, but all my life Mother's been telling me about the covenant. At midnight. By the fire with the stars. Like summer camp, Dad. And you promised. To the sacred dark. We took care of ourselves, my grandparents, mother, and I, but now . . ." I had to stop. I might need the bucket after all.

"Are you all right, man?" he shouted. "Two legs. Two eyes?"

"I'm much too tall."

"Me too."

"And, Dad, I hate all this sex." So many years I'd wanted to talk to him.

He laughed just like a father. "Good. Keep you out of trouble 'til the right time comes. Then you'll be like Vinnie and love it."

"But right now you've got to help us."

His voice grew softer. I was watching Mother and I knew she could still hear him. "Elisabeth, I don't do women and children any more."

"That's all right."

I wasn't trying to be polite; I'm never polite. Somehow I knew what he had said didn't matter; but that something else did and that right now, on the phone with Jacob, calling Jacob in New Hampshire, I had to figure out what did.

I was still struggling with what mattered, trying to remember what Mother had taught me, when he shouted, "Elisabeth?"

"I'm thinking. I'm thinking it's O.K. about no more women and children, but how are you as a person?"

I wanted to ask, "Do you giggle and squeak like Bittsie?" but I didn't know my own father well enough for that.

"Elisabeth." His voice was soft again. "I was just a kid."

"Jacob, you must be grown up by now."

He said, "Elisabeth, you're a together kid."

Mother pulled out her handkerchief. Mr. Folsom swiveled his chair around and stared at the wall. Then we all heard Jacob say very slowly, "Maybe the jeep can wait."

I gave him our address and then I said, "I'd really like to meet you someday, Jacob."

We both hung up.

"Well." Mr. Folsom swung his chair back facing me. "Well, then, Elisabeth, would you consider joining my firm?"

I reached for my comb. Mother reached for me, saying, "You're my miracle baby."

I said, "Maybe."

▪ Brotherhood ▪

Mother's Day. 1982. There was a long line of cars at the cemetery gate.

Maybe I failed to hear Brother John. Maybe he did not say where he was taking me. Perhaps he thought, "Three martinis, Jasper'll never know."

Nonsense.

I always know where I am going. I always know where I have been. I would never have been in John's car, waiting in line at Memorial Park with flowers for Mother's grave, if John had not tricked me. I hate cemeteries. Any real man does when he gets to be sixty-four.

That car John loves—comfortable as a kangaroo's pouch—jumped forward. My head hit the windshield. "John," I said, "keep this up and you'll be tucking me under a headstone." Not that I will ever have one, but if I were to, it would have a single word on it: "NO." Someone has to keep protesting.

John and I look alike. Six-feet-two. Grizzling hair. "Ermine eyebrows," he used to say. "Skunk-striped," I would answer. Stiff straight backs. Stiff straight noses. Stiff straight lips. Still no hanging stomachs, but my chin is falling. Any morning I could wake up looking like a pelican.

John once said we resembled John L. Lewis and tilted our cigarettes like F.D.R. Mygod.

My twin brother is up to his ermine eyebrows in psychofaddle. ESP. Meditation. Yoga. Truth through beets and vitamin C. Talking about your feelings. Hugging.

Brotherhood. Rain or shine he does headstands on his balcony by Lake Michigan.

He always uses a soft, sliding voice when he is trying to do somebody good, and his slightly protruding eyes go deep and teary. At the cemetery that day, his voice seemed to be quivering from middle C to high C. Sitting like a flyboy in a Ramon Navarro film, he gripped the steering wheel as if he were getting ready for a difficult take-off. He mumbled something about "problem" and "at Mother's grave." He seemed to say, "talk it out together."

I did not answer. No reason to howl because I was not sure what he said. With my new glasses I see more than I ever did. Smells are sharper now. I know wines better than John ever will. I have more time to read. I walked more briskly than John until that damned day at the cemetery.

"I wish you'd go for help. Learn to be happy." His voice slid back to middle C and he stressed *wish* to show he cared. The car motor rumbled and complained. He began to shout, and his voice beat against the cartop, mingled with the car sounds, rattled the windows, and came back to me like blows on the head. I think he said, "There's a young woman, a counselor at the Senior Center. Damned fine. I wish you'd talk to her."

"John, I don't need some ninny to tell me how to think and live. I've read all the books she has. Freud. Jung. Breuer. Menninger. Fromm. *I'm OK—You're OK. How to Live with Yourself and Not Vomit.*"

I heard his answer but my ears made a mishmash of the words. I interrupted. "I know my problem. I know how to deal with it. If I start talking all over town, I might kill someone. Maybe you."

He said, "You're mumbling."

The car moved forward on the gravel drive. The tips of his fingers paled on the steering wheel. His right hand moved to the shift, his hands eased, and the car shook itself like a furred animal about to leap. He smiled sweetly. Shifting gears is one of his hobbies.

Something I took to be music seeped from the cemetery chapel. The sun on the hot metal of the slow-moving cars gave off a musty scent tinged with the limey smell of fresh cement. We moved slowly past a new columbarium. Columbarium. Mygod.

He turned to face me, spacing out the words, chewing each one like gristle. "Jasper, I worry about you."

"Drop it, John. I'm not one of your projects."

John's brain has been spongy ever since Mother read us *Little Lord Fauntleroy*. I had trouble with the Little Lord for a while myself. I thought I was a poet. Law school and the big-bang war killed that. I still do my club's Christmas letter. In verse, of course. Not poetry.

Before he could urge his toy into another hop, I opened the car door and started back to the entrance. Widows wailed. Children patted dirt or wandered beyond the tombstones, picking dandelions. Fools, all of them. No one was waiting for their visit. I should have patted each lonely widowed bottom.

Twenty, thirty, forty years ago, I would have tiptoed through the tombstones like Fred Astaire. Three martinis. Five martinis. No matter. Still, because of my new glasses I went carefully. My feet felt loose. Then, suddenly, the black, familiar anger enwrapped me. I walked faster. Earth had sunk away from a headstone. I tripped. Two chipmunks emerged from a hole by the grave, sending open-mouthed children scurrying to their mothers. My back twisted like a pretzel and I fell. My right leg splintered.

John followed the ambulance to the hospital, and here I am at his tender loving mercy twenty-seven minutes every afternoon. Three-o-three until three-thirty. Every day.

The nurses spoil me. They cluck-cluck like friendly fowl. Their buttocks weave parabolas of inexorable splendor. The night nurse sometimes smells of semen. Hospitals are cheerful now, pink as ice cream cones. My leg and hip— something wrong there too—are suspended over my bed like a side of beef hung up to age. The sun through the blinds at the window traces bars across my hospital gown.

Three-o-three. John as usual. He is trim still and wears leftover Brooks tweeds and a school tie. He may claim jogging gives him a high, live in a small apartment, and drive a German kangaroo, but he still dresses like a gentleman.

"Tired of being nibbled to death by midgets," he wrote me in London when he retired at fifty-seven. "I'd rather live poor and happy."

He still has his clubs, but he cannot afford to lunch at them. He says he is keeping them for his obituary.

He writes YES on my cast with a big, pink, soft pencil. That is short for "Say YES to life." John is a great yea-sayer. To be fair he sometimes says, "Yes?"

He pulls up a chair and leans close to me. His tongue pushes and thrusts. He twists his lips like a squirrel worrying a nut. After a while he shouts, "Aren't you going to answer me?"

"I am always willing to answer," I say, "provided I know what's being said."

He puts on his Saint Sebastian face, making clear his sorrow for me—my life, my drinking, the success he says turned me ruthless.

He could do with less ruth. The Little Lord would have made a miserable lawyer.

What can I answer? Sorry I live better than you and have room for the ancestral portraits? Please excuse me for marrying better, lawyering better, and having plenty of trusts to administer. My apologies for driving a Mercedes. For not spilling my guts at the Local League for the Aged.

We sit silent. A slight smile freezes his lips. He is being patient. Good, faithful, sanctimonious John. Only he knows my rage. Now that he has me trussed up with pulleys and wire, he is sure to try me again with his young psychologist friend.

She comes the next day. She has metallic lips and a dimple. A one-two-three smile. At the count of one the upper lip rises over tombstone teeth. On the count of two the upper left-hand corner of her glossy mouth quirks. Count three and the dimple on her left cheek deepens. She pats my hand. She coos. One-two-three-pat-coo.

I note three things in her favor. She speaks slowly and her knees dimple sweetly. She would look like a magazine cover if only she would unbutton that blue blouse.

I tell her I have always made my own mistakes. I say, "I'm too old to change."

"Why? You've only one life to live. Why not enjoy?"

"And be like my brother John?"

"You're not being totally honest with yourself. Maybe if you talked about how you feel . . ." She smells like a pizza.

"I'd rather discuss Heisenberg's concept of uncertainty." There's time for that at the hospital, nothing but time, hung up in my prison stripes. Outside my window the pale green leaves of the treetops are still faintly curled. Beyond them squats the fluted white dome of the Bahai temple. Orange juice squeezer for anybody's god.

Dimples says, "You could try making it easier for others."

"You don't even know me."

"I do now."

"You live your life. I'll live mine. Before you go I'd like to kiss your knees."

Prim as a deaconess, she shakes her head and goes.

I wonder whom John will send next.

The next afternoon his minister has a try at me. Waterfall beard. Rosy cheeks and bright blue eyes. His tweeds sag and his socks are red. His message is as nauseant as Dimples's: Love. Beauty. Wisdom. Harmony. Brotherhood. Joy. His sort of priest is very big on joy.

I say, "I may have lost my faith, but I haven't lost my mind."

He leans back and waggles a finger at me. He laughs a long time. Then he talks. And talks. I suffocate in the perfume of his bay rum until John comes. The minister probably tells him it has been a joy to meet me. He rolls out, buoyant as a rubber fish. One more participant in John's conspiracy of cheer.

When John finally leaves, I begin to reread *The Decline and Fall*. I read Gibbon every fifth spring. Upperclass Romans knew how to bear adversity. I would like to turn on the television during dinner, but not knowing what anybody is saying makes me angry. I even reach for the telephone, then put it down without dialing. Telephones are useless to me now. I twist and turn until the sheets wrinkle under me, as comfortable as the pebbled beach I lay on during an Indian dig. My hospital sheets smell of bleach.

I close my eyes.

In the darkness behind my eyes, my wife lies dying, smiling, pretending to be happy. Ten years have passed, but I can still see the white room, the white bed, and the red roses I had brought. It was evening and the shadows were gathering around her. I held her hand. Her head was like a skull—bones as elegant as a Hogarth etching—black hair tied in a knot with a red velvet ribbon, fingers spread to hide the gap where a tooth had been. She seemed to say words we did not know when we were young together. I longed to hear her soft voice again, but I was new then to the world of meaningless sounds and did not know how to help her speak to me. I kissed her dry lips and went to bed with a book. Unanswered, she died.

I lie here, remembering, and begin to understand my parents. All through John's and my school years, we would talk for hours around the big dinner table. Politics. Art. Religion. Physics. Words, phrases, metaphors, puns dipped and rose, glittering like the spangled chandelier over our heads. There was no need to spell out each thought, nor to say each word aloud. We understood each other. We interrupted. We corrected. We embellished.

I do not want to think of Mother again, but as the days pass, I do. In our talks, she was the quickest of us all. Did the universe begin with a bang? Or was it the result of a chemical accident, like people? Was it still expanding? Jasper, explain the Black Hole theory. How can Zola be called a naturalistic writer when he left out all the good? No, that was not Mother. It was Brother John, soft in the head even then. "John," Mother said, "Zola made it seem that even the bad could be made good. I like that."

Sometime after the war Mother stopped talking. She sat silent with her needlepoint, smiling, tsk-tsking as we refilled our glasses. Once she said, "I like watching my men talk." She did not often hazard more lest Father shout, "But weren't you listening?" Or, "You heard me, dear." Sometimes he said, "But I was speaking very clearly." Or, "If you'd only listen, dear."

Libbers would have something to say about that *dear*. I agree, but I liked the old feminists better. They worked harder. They did not scream through their noses. They did not discuss their sex habits. Would they have understood why Father slapped the table and swore? Why Mother held him in her arms as if he were the one who had lost his hearing? Why I stopped going home unless I was sure Father would not be there?

In my poet-days, I used to compare Mother's aging to the wild cherry tree near our summer home. Frail and greenly fair. Webworms wrapped the tree in a shining shroud patterned by the sun. Grubs fed inside, six to twenty to a leaf, as gregarious as sorrows. Storms tore the web. Dust grayed the silken strands. Birds fouled it with their droppings. The grubs fed on and the leaves clotted in filth. When all the leaves were gone, the tree died.

I was damned lyric in those days. Editors called my poems "adolescent."

Mother died beating her fists against the bars of her bed. It was a bed like mine in this same hospital.

I used to spit every time I passed the old home place on Sheridan Road. I would spit on Father's grave, but for that I would have to go back to Memorial Park.

Someday I may forgive my father. A bastard, yes, but that was the way he was trained. John and I were no better at helping Mother hear. Nonetheless, I still believe in hate. It is better than squash racquets or tennis for keeping the blood flowing, a man's way to clear out the dry rot of sentimentality.

No one but John knows my hatred. A gentleman hides his emotions.

Still, lying here in the hospital, I remember John's saying, "Mother should have spoken up more. Made Dad understand." I had not known how to explain to my wife. Maybe I have not tried hard enough to teach John how to speak to me. I need to know what is being said. Always. Anywhere. Not just a word now and then.

I open my book, but Gibbon is gloomy; and so I pull my checkbook from the table by my bed. I write my annual checks.

To the Princeton Alumni Fund.

To Jasper Hall. One of Mother's granddaddies built it.

To the Republican National Committee. No matter that in the White House some forked-carrot idiot is smiling his aw-shucks smile.

To Seaman's Rest. Father's great-great-grandfather founded it.

To Planned Parenthood. The wrong people keep having brats.

To the Lyric Opera and Ravinia. Some people still enjoy music. John uses my box at the symphony.

To Saint Andrew's Society. Once a year I wear my kilts and eat haggis. I used to like bagpipes.

To the Episcopal Diocese. Belief aside, the church soothes and stabilizes. I like the ritual.

Usually I wait until December to write these checks. I know then precisely the deductions I need.

What I am really doing is waiting for John.

Three-o-three and he is back. Gray sweater. Gray slacks. Gray Harris tweed jacket. Thin red tie. A damned good-looking man. He has brought a radio. His slim fingers fuss at it as if he were working the controls of a giant switchboard. Higher and higher goes the volume until I put my hands to my ears. I have never been able to convince him that our beloved Mozart is now like knives in my head.

Still, my brother has come.

He screws up his lips and mouths his words. He snaps his fingers at me and shakes his head. I understand most of it. "Have a good lunch?" "Can you sleep hung up like that?" "Going to rain?" Even intelligent people talk that way to the hard of hearing. Then he cocks his head and waits for my response to this brilliant conversational ploy.

Good old John. He always does the best he can. His friends still like him. His sons still like him.

The nurses and the hospital must have softened me. Maybe having a hip and leg hung up to cure changed my perspective, as John says his headstands do. It seems to me that John and I have stepped into that Goya painting, two men up to their hips in sand, fighting with cudgels to the death. I do not want to live the rest of my life hip-deep in sand.

"John," I say, "you were always a fool, but . . ."

Tapered fingers cup his ear. His breathing grows quick, but he smiles still. "Speak up, speak up," he says, and I know then that John too grows deaf.

Like Mother. Like me.

Grayness and filth close in on me; the webworms feed on. The winding sheet of my rage tightens as I lunge for my brother. "Go home, John," I say, and as he pulls back, I am falling again, this time in a jangle of wires and buckles, pulleys and pain, still shouting, as broken plaster falls with me, "Go home and stand on your head."

◼ "I Don't Understand You," She Said ◼

The first call came to his desk at the *Sun-Times* in late September. "Mr. Willowby? Northbrook police. We've got your wife."

Her name was Joyce, but she had always been called Joy; when she laughed, everyone laughed.

She'd been lunching with Effie Stanton at Northbrook Court, Jack knew that much. The two friends—Effie in black hose, miniskirt, and jersey, and Joy, a large woman with a swing to her step, in sweeping red corduroy and heavy silver jewelry—would lunch every month or so and talk for hours. Then they strolled from store to store. Joy never bought much, and when she did, it was always "because it was on sale."

The officer made it sound as if Joy were drunk, but Joy never drank in the daytime and never drank without him. Effie drank nonalcoholic champagne at New Year's Eve parties.

Jack reached the mall in forty minutes against the wind, too fast even for Edens Expressway. Joy was huddled in her tan Olds, a policewoman at her side. He held his wife until she recognized him.

Her voice was like a child's. "Effie remembered she had to be home early and she ran off. I wandered around, Jack. I bought a dress I've been wanting, but all that noise, Jack, lights flashing, escalators going up and down—I couldn't remember where I'd left the car. I just walked and walked and someone was playing, 'Do it, Do it,' and that dress in the bag skittered in the wind until I lost it.

"Jack, I couldn't remember my car."

The officer beckoned and Jack met her behind the Olds.

"May I suggest a checkup? She really was lost."

"She's in perfect health."

"Mr. Willowby, believe me."

"We jog every morning."

"Right away, sir."

They went back to Joy and the policewoman said, "Mrs. Willowby, your husband has agreed to take you to a doctor."

"I go every spring."

"As soon as possible."

Suddenly Joy's tears were gone. "He's the one who needs a doctor. After what he's done to me."

He took her home and called the garage to pick up the Olds. (It wasn't until the next day that he realized there was nothing wrong with the Olds and that he'd have to ask the garage to bring it back to Joy.) He poured Chardonnay and sat beside her, looking out at her prize chrysanthemums, seeing colors he had not seen since they were young and smoked together. Red on flamingo on scarlet, yellow and green on gold.

"You planned it all," he said. "Maples and firs against the oaks." He raised his glass. "We've been happy here."

"I don't understand you at all," she said.

He stroked her hand. "Can you tell me what I've done?"

"You're never here."

"I'm always here. Unless I'm writing or chasing a story."

"That being all the time."

"You like your own time, your own thing."

"Please, dear," she said.

"I can't make it right unless I know what's wrong."

"I don't want to talk." Her voice echoed as if their house were suddenly empty.

Then, because she had always liked to hear about his mail, he said, "One of my fans wrote to suggest I give up column-writing and get a job with Deep Tunnel."

She said, "I don't understand you at all."

Explaining killed any wit there might have been in sewage control versus muck-raking; and so, as they had always loved to do, they sat knee to knee with their books. An hour later, he read her a paragraph from Tom Hayden. She said, "You keep interrupting. It's incredible the way you talk."

At ten she put down *The Old Man and the Sea*. (When she'd first read it in *Life*, she said, "Jack, don't ever let our life be like that.") Her fingers marched up his thigh. She said, "I want to make love *for* you."

In bed she balanced on stiffened arms above him. "You look like a newspaper man."

"You used to say I looked like an SDS."

"Same difference. All that hair. Your nose is good, but the rest of your face looks as if God's knife slipped." She lowered herself slowly and kissed the tip of his nose. "Love you much."

She was like a young girl, but she'd learned a trick or two in their twenty years of marriage, never mind the *wanderjahr* before. Their bodies linked; their mouths joined; the old words came. "Sweet. Sweet." His tongue probed deep, and the current broke. He clung to her. "Comebackcomeback."

She said, "Whoever you are, you fuck good."

He had not heard her use that word in twenty years.

He lay awake and remembered that she could not really have been reading Hemingway. Some of the pages of their first edition were overprinted and unreadable.

He thought of family legends: her great-grandmother, barely five feet tall, searching the Highland Park ravines for her six-foot-four father who was walking home to Troy, New York. *His* great-grandmother, teaching her only son that making love was like losing a pint of blood. For a full three minutes he wondered if the Victorian doctor who had taught her that might have been right.

Finally, to ease the worm that gnawed his belly, he went to his study and put five pages into his computer. He walked back and forth until at seven Joy came to find him to jog.

Saturday they were going to walk in the woods and he couldn't find his red wool shirt. He opened Joy's closet and there, this Saturday morning, among the tulip-colored dresses—red, orange, purple, and pink—were six black party dresses still in their plastic bags with price tags.

They had not gone to a dress-up party since Joy had given up selling real estate.

"I'm through with that."

"I thought you liked helping people nest."

"Not really."

"We'll miss the money."

"I made enough."

"We spent it."

Just two years ago, knee to knee, he'd said, "I don't want to spend my life writing daily stuff. I don't want to write any more sperm-*und*-druck suspense. I want to finish my novel."

"How many chapters?"

"Ten. And twenty notebooks. I've got it now. Why we believed. SDS versus the old Socialists versus the Maoists."

"Vis-à-vis the Ho Chi Minh people."

"And the Establishment."

"Don't forget the Libidinists," she had said. "Every serious novel has to have sex."

"I want to tell about us before I forget how I felt."

"So this is a novel with labels?"

"No. People. Good people."

"Then I'll gladly pay the bills."

"It's your book too," he said. "Our life."

Joy had been the perfect wife for a columnist in need of a new story every day. People told her their most intimate traumas while meditating the dimensions of a bedroom. Friends called at midnight and said, "I have to talk to you." Joy used to be a psychic vacuum cleaner, pulling in stories for him.

Everyone wanted to be on her committees, to act in the Community House plays she directed, to be part of her jokes. One year, six couples hired a bus to go with them to the Arts Ball in Chicago. They stood in the aisle all the way, a swaying, stumbling mass of green and yellow stripes, so they could disembark, to loud applause, as a centipede.

Some stepped back when she began her wild, rambling, resonant talk. Teenagers fled. The strong used her competence and enthusiasm. Jack always had.

Standing there, staring at the new dresses, he realized he hadn't missed the parties. He'd been too busy distilling jokes from political speeches, too involved trying to rouse the staff against a takeover by someone he called "The Cockney Princeling."

(There had been threats. "Go ahead," he had written, "bomb. My computer's old.")

Once, feeling Joy must be missing downtown theater and dinners, he'd planned a day in the city with her. "No, thanks," she had said, "I've been to Chicago."

A voice—all resonance lost—interrupted his thoughts. "Jack, you're snooping."

"My Bean shirt," he said, and then, "Why all the dresses?"

"They were on sale."

Sunday he completed chapter twelve and doodled page after page of titles: *The Young Believers. We Were Right to Believe. Candide and Company. Peace Was Not Always a Dirty Word. Even Reagan Says "Peace" Now. The Sixties Look Different When You Get to Be Forty. I Believe in Money Now. Where Did We All Go?*

Joy came in several times and emptied the wastebasket. When he looked up she gave him a basset-hound stare, as if to say, "How could you?"

He went down at six. Joy was on the bottom step, reading scraps from his wastebasket.

The doctors said she needed counseling. She no longer walked with a swing and a bounce, but she seemed more alert, almost at ease. It was his gut that ached. Each time she caught him taking a pill, she said, "I really don't think you need that."

He let himself hope, even when Effie called and apologized for leaving Joy at the mall.

"I couldn't stand it," she said. "Not Joy."

A week later he realized Joy was still reading *The Old Man and the Sea.*

"How come Hemingway?"

"Why not?"

"No reason. I wondered if you were planning to make a play of it. Small boat awash in blue sheets. Joy Willowby at the helm."

"I don't understand you at all."

Ten days before Halloween she said, "Jack, you've got to talk to Effie. Tell her I don't want her dropping in all the time."

"You tell her. She's your friend."

"She snoops."

He did not say he'd berated her friend. He did not repeat Effie's advice: Lower your expectations.

Joy joined a club called Sweet Sweat. She had a massage three afternoons a week. Those nights she was eager for sex. Night after night he held her until she slept. Night after night he worked at his desk, emptying a can of peanuts as he drank. Sometimes at dawn, his upper lip prickling from the bourbon, he walked to the beach to let the water—gray, blue, turquoise—quiet him.

He tried to tell Joy why he couldn't sleep.

He said, "We never talk."

He said, "You seem to have walked away."

He said, "We're too young for this."

He said, "I'm lonely without you."

He asked, "Is it because of the IUD? Because we can't have kids?"

He asked, "What can I do to help?"

She said, "I don't understand you at all."

Those last months, as he waited for the doctors to tell him what to do, his column seemed to wound only himself. He erased chapter twenty; it read like an apology.

Joy worked in the garden, pulling plants, trimming, clipping. When everything seemed ready for winter, she dug up the vegetable garden again. Then again. One Saturday he found her holding a clod of dirt, staring at it, as if to ask what she must do with it. When the weather turned too chill for outdoor work, she watched television all day. In the evening, he sat beside her, touching her hand, ready for the old mockery: the world is mad but we know how to laugh. She did not respond. She had a musty smell.

In December he urged her to give their annual New Year's Eve party.

"I don't need those people."

"Please, dear, try."

He arranged for catered food. Joy polished the silver candlesticks, a gift from her mother. She had her hair cut and tinted a premature apricot. (Last year she'd laughed at his surprise that so many graying women at the *Sun-Times* had turned apricot.) She wore one of the new black dresses—pouffed and three inches above her knees—with a ruffled white organdy tie-back from their bedroom curtains as a bracelet.

Just as he had hoped, she seemed buoyed by the mem-

ory of parties past. He helped refill platters with shrimp
and crab and oysters. She had made a vegetable casserole
with brown rice for Effie. In the kitchen, Joy whispered,
"These parties. We need name tags. I seem to have lost
mine." He left her then and took Tom Stanton to his study
for a private drink; he was still avoiding Effie. At ten, on
their way back to the party, they met Joy in the upper hall.
"May I go to bed now?"

Joy had put away the food and wine. She had washed
the dishes and crystal and returned everything to the cup-
boards. She had snuffed the candles. Tom, at his side,
said, "You're a zombie yourself. You're not seeing because
you don't want to."

Half an hour later, Joy shuffled through the guests in
her sheer nightgown. "My glasses," she said. "I can't find
my glasses."

They had all seen her in a bathing suit. Some of them
had seen her without. "A Picasso woman," Jack loved to
say. "Large and soft and pink and proud of it." This was
different. She was not in control of her nakedness. Her
nightdress was soiled.

Everyone went home before midnight.

Yesterday Joy met him at the train and they drove down
Green Bay Road to pick up her car, which had been in the
shop for a smashed fender. He waited to make sure she
did not skid on the icy street. She backed out fast and
before he could honk, hit a red truck. Without a pause,
she took the Olds back into the shop. On their way home
at last, he said, "I'll take the keys. No more driving."

She did not object. "My psychiatrist wants to see you
tomorrow afternoon. Alone. I didn't forget. I just hated to
tell you. Because it's your fault."

He hid in the study and called Effie. She said, "We used
to discuss free will long into the night. When we weren't
arguing political strategy. I can't remember if you believed.

If Joy believed. Either way, this is where it stops for Joy."

"She keeps blaming me."

"Because you're there."

"Maybe I am to blame. I forget her sometimes when I'm working. I let her drive into that truck. Because I didn't want to stop her driving and make her unhappy. Two feet more, she'd have killed herself. Maybe that's what I hoped."

He said, "I miss her so."

The psychiatrist could have been his son. He said, "It's chemical. That's all we know. We call it loss of self. No one is to blame."

For a moment Jack's pain eased. There was a name for what was happening to them and it wasn't his fault.

The psychiatrist said, "Take care of yourself. We'll help if we can. She's not unhappy."

"Please, God." Jack had not said that word for thirty years.

It was not yet five, but beyond the office window a pinkish sky was turning black as a bruise. He seemed to have found himself again. A man like any other. A man who kept making mistakes. An aging man who loved his wife and could not help her. A man young enough to learn to reject the words, "It's your fault."

He was not really listening as the young doctor explained what lay ahead. He was thinking that, no matter what, he would keep working during his sleepless nights. Despite all loss, he would finish his book. Their book.

The doctor was saying, "She'll probably wander at night. Get new locks. We'll give her something. We can't promise it will help."

◾

◼ Heritage Clay ◼

She sensed Julian come in, but remembering the party at the Officer's Club, remembering too that for the first time in their long marriage he had gone into the guest room and shut the door (he was not one to slam), she did not speak or get up. She was lying at the base of a revolving stand—the north light of her studio clear and bright—looking up at a working model of her statue and assessing the bulk of the woman's heavy socks. On the wall behind her hung one red wool sock. Her plaster model of a woman running wore the other.

Standing above her, he asked, "Must she be so thin and sad?"

The clay figure wore a tattered T-shirt, jeans, socks, and tennis shoes with a toe protruding. She held up her shirt with one hand. Her round belly hung low. Yesterday Dorothy had stripped away the woman's hair and tapped the bare skull with a mallet to simulate nappy hair. ("If only mine could be like that.") Three children huddled at the statue's feet.

"Yes," Dorothy said, "she's a survivor."

They'd quarreled about survivors. "We must keep Fort Sheridan open," Julian (Captain, United States Coast Guard Retired) had been saying to his Navy friends at the party. "For survivors."

"What survivors?" she'd asked.

"Civilians," Julian had said in his command voice. "We're talking about the evacuation of survivors in case of nuclear attack."

"Just so they have shovels," Dorothy had said.

119

Now, moving closer to the statue, Julian said, "She'll get thinner in the rain."

"This one will be cast in bronze." Even now she couldn't believe that her husband paid so little attention to the process of her work.

He pulled her to her feet and led her to a chair by the big window. "Every time I open my mouth you oppose me."

"Yes," she said.

She didn't believe Star Wars meant peace. She didn't believe nuclear plants should be built until scientists figured out what to do with the waste. She didn't believe the government should decide who might have an abortion. She did not believe . . .

"I would ask you, Dorothy, not to challenge me in front of my friends. They're professionals. They know what they're talking about."

"I have to say what I feel."

"You weren't so opinionated when I married you."

"When we married."

"Think what you must." He spoke slowly. "But at the officer's parties, please shut up."

"Touch me," she said. "Please." But she didn't say it aloud.

He said, "I suppose your statue is protecting her children from me," and walked away.

Her fingers caressed her statue. She pressed her thumbs into the woman's forehead. Her beloved clay was soft and cool and oily. Her mother had willed her the clay. Heritage clay. Ninety years old. "It will mold your life," her mother had said. Now Dorothy's life threatened the clay. Her hand was too heavy.

She stood for a moment studying the scale model of the park where her statue would stand, then sprayed the figures with quick wide arcs of water. She wrung out cloths from the water bucket, wrapped the woman and her children, then washed and dried her tools. On her way to the car, she put cheese and an apple in her tote. Just this once she'd break working rules and go downtown during the day. Just this once she'd march for a Nuclear Free Zone no matter how Julian might feel.

Julian had been a conscientious objector before Pearl Harbor. (They'd talked all that night. "At least I should defend our coasts.") His first assignment was Dakar. He'd seen ships go down for lack of equipment and well-trained men; he'd do and think as the Coast Guard brass did until he died. Dorothy sent cash to peace groups in anonymous brown envelopes.

Julian was the one with friends. Dorothy was prickly and abrasive, or so his friends thought. Julian remembered names, cared about other people's children, and asked about hobbies. Despite a hip that made him limp, he stood straight and never complained. ("It's getting worse fast," the doctors had told Dorothy.) He'd given up sailing, but he still preferred cruises and tramp steamers to any other ways of travel.

His blue eyes got bluer as his hair grayed. He wore deep blue blazers, bright blue ties, and gray flannels even when mowing the lawn. He swerved for turtles on the road and stopped for sunsets. Three days a week he read to patients at the Navy hospital. He gave two or three lectures a month and regularly hosted a round-table luncheon for Chicago's leading journalists.

As for Dorothy, sailing weekends had given her wrinkles. She'd never liked boats or ships, but as she said on their last cruise of the Virgin Islands, "Julian is the only husband I have." The wrinkles gave her face the translucence of parchment.

Long ago one of Julian's tizzled friends who pinched her at parties said, "Dorothy, as far as looks go, you don't have much to work with, but I admire what you do with it." She'd thrown away her makeup and pulled her hair to the side in a ponytail. For parties she tied a ribbon over the rubber band. She bought heavy eyelashes. (No matter that she imitated Louise Nevelson; her sculptures were not like Nevelson's.) As she traveled with Julian she collected handwoven skirts. She'd gone bra-less since the sixties, but sometimes her scoop-necked blouses slipped to reveal the grooves in her shoulders made by twenty years of bra-wearing. Thong sandals showed off her long toes ("Well, you do have beautiful feet") until it was the season for boots. On the days when her plain brown hair didn't get clay in it, Julian's friends pronounced her "arty" and "statuesque."

Still, even the service wives who agreed with her didn't want lectures at their dinner tables. Only her fellow artists and three of her four children liked her quick tongue. Only Julian knew that she still trembled at his touch.

"NO MORE NUKES. NO MORE NUKES."

In front of the State of Illinois Building, flags and banners flew as men and women with baby buggies and baby packs, in wheelchairs and on walkers, wove in and out of the Dubuffet statue. (Julian called it "Fire Sale—charred at the edges.") A thin pale man on a bicycle—he looked like a messenger—circled the marchers three times, calling, "Right on." Dorothy walked up to a woman she didn't know and shook her hand. Then, chanting, she entered the line of marchers. A man in a Burberry cap and raincoat, a slim briefcase in his hand, leaned toward her. She expected him to say, "Thank you," or maybe, "Join me later for a drink?" Instead he whispered, "Fuck you enough, you'd shut up."

She swung her fist and struck softness. His face suddenly turned gray. Retching, he bent over and clutched his stomach. She turned back across Daley Plaza, barely missing the young messenger on his bicycle and ran through the noontime crowd, past the Picasso, then east to Michigan Avenue. A brisk September wind blew her ponytail across her eyes as, head down, she walked north. She didn't know whether to laugh or shout. For the first time since she was a child, she had struck someone. Would he go to the police? Perhaps a reporter would visit her at the Cook County Jail. (CAPTAIN'S WIFE KO'S LOOP ATTORNEY. PACIFIST COAST GUARD WIFE JAILED ON ASSAULT CHARGES.) "Yes," she'd say, "yes, I hit him and I'm glad."

She ate lunch by the lake, near Oak Street beach. Above cobalt waters, white clouds roamed a Cezanne sky. She pulled her sketchbook from her tote bag. Page after page of studies for the mother: stubby feet, shoulders in a crouch, the interior of the skull. Within the mother's skull, in subtle harmony, bone lay into bone. But why would the mother want to live and give birth to a child, when all around her, men and women struck out at strangers because they were unhappy?

The shadows by the shore deepened into indigo. Two sailboats tacked north, parallel to each other and to the shore. Years ago at a Republican meeting, she'd learned that she and Julian had to live parallel lives. At the meeting, she'd heckled the speaker and questioned his facts. Later she heard Julian on the telephone, apologizing.

She might not like sailing, but now, watching the boats, so far yet so close, one to another, she remembered: Never cross a friend's bow. Julian would not change his course. Nor would she. If only she could keep her own rules . . .

By midafternoon, she was heading back down Michigan. The sun and water had done their healing. A heaviness had fallen from her eyes. Everyone she saw seemed of heroic size, waiting for her sketchbook and her clay: A middle-aged woman in blue serge, a lace hanky in her pocket, hopped to keep in step with the man at her side. A beardless youngster leaned against the Tribune Tower and nodded off. Men in matching gray suits and yellow ties walked five abreast. An elderly gentleman in navy pinstripes cradled a silvery Persian cat in his arms.

At South Water, a black man with spiked hair handed her a paper. Hand out, palm up, he said, "Five . . . ?"

"No money," she said. "I'll read it first."

His hand was on hers. He kissed the knuckles. Then standing as far from her as possible to reassure her, he shook her hand, turned it and shook hands again, touched thumbs, and finally locked fingers. "Thank you, thank you," he said. At the top of the mimeograph handout was the Lord's Prayer. Under a smudged picture of children with swollen bellies was a request for "land, bread, housing, education, clothing, justice, and peace for World Africans."

Land? Bread? Housing and education? Clothing, justice, and peace? She read the words again. Only the basics, right?

If, in truth, there were a goddess mother in some celestial daycare center ("O.K., kids, everyone gets to use the finger paints.") was she making plans?

Land, bread, housing . . . The mother was probably looking right at her, saying in her patient voice, "You all have to help. One step at a time."

Dorothy wasn't a believer, but thinking about the goddess made her feel stronger.

She turned back and gave the petitioner a bill. ("I know, Julian, he'll probably buy a bottle.") Behind her, down the block, brakes screeched.

At the intersection to the south, the pale rider who had called out encouragement to the marchers was turning west. His wheels slipped and he fell in front of a red pickup truck. As he rose, the driver leapt into the street and knocked him down, then picked up the bicycle and slammed it to the pavement. The rider retrieved his packet of messages and reached for his bicycle. The larger man lifted it again and beat it against the pavement. Pieces of metal scattered. She could not hear what the messenger said, but his gesture was universal: "Now, let's be reasonable."

How pale he was. She wanted to call out, "Stop. Let me sketch you just so."

The rider wrote down the truck's license number. The driver lunged and ripped the young man's jacket. The smaller man backed away. The other followed. No one on the sidewalk seemed to see them. There was no policeman.

They were near her now, necks protruding in Neanderthal fashion, no sound between them, only the eyes, the cold eyes that said, "I'll kill you" and "I'll fight as long as I can."

The larger man smiled. His heavy suede jacket was tight over heavy muscles. He had a scar over one eye. Shrapnel? A bullet? The pale young man's breathing was heavy and frayed. His left foot caught in a break in the sidewalk. His ankle turned. He did not look down. He did not miss a step. The other, his face dull and red, kept coming. Eye to eye, neither one able to look away, it was as if they were chained together. Dorothy stepped between them. The larger man's breath mingled with hers. She felt his body heat. She said, "Time to stop now." The larger man blinked. Eye contact broke. The anger broke. Both shouted obscenities. They shuffled their feet, shook sweat from their eyes, and walked away. As he passed her, the pale young man said, "Thank you, mam."

Dorothy hurries now, heading for her car, for home, for Julian. Just one more time she will veer from her course.

She will tell him, "I broke the chain of violence." ("Please shut up," he'd said.) Then, sails spread before the wind, she will shape her own course.

Tomorrow she will add strips of gray-green clay to the mother's belly. Tomorrow she will model the baby inside, one leg out, as if stepping from the womb, eager, despite everything, to be born.

■